KT-495-993

# ALL~TIME FAVOURITE CLASSICS

BRIMAR

© 1998 Disney Enterprises, Inc.
Illustrations: Kodansha Ltd.
Graphic design: Zapp

Produced and published by
Brimar Publishing Inc.
338 Saint Antoine St. East
Montreal, Canada H2Y 1A3
Tel. (514) 954-1441
Fax (514) 954-5086

ISBN 2-89433-373-0

Printed in the U.S.A.

# CONTENTS

Based on the book by Dodie Smith. Published by Heinemann Ltd.

Hi! My name is Pongo. This story began one beautiful spring day. Roger, my pet, was busy trying to write a song. He's a musician, and practically married to his work.

I thought life would be more interesting if we had a companion. So I was looking out the window for a suitable mate. Two really – one for Roger, and one for me.

That's when I saw her – a beautiful Dalmatian. Her human looked nice, too. "Perfect!" I decided.

It took some quick thinking to get Roger away from his work. But soon I was able to convince him to go for a walk.

I spotted them as soon as we entered the park. The Dalmatian was named Perdita. She was wonderful!

But as usual, Roger had his head in the clouds. He barely noticed Perdita's human, Anita. Sometimes I wonder about these human beings.

Finally, I wound my leash around their legs, and tipped them into the pond. That got them to notice each other! It also got Perdita to notice me.

Well, before long, Roger asked Anita to marry him, and Perdita agreed to marry me, too. It was a beautiful double wedding.

After that, our house became a paradise for dogs and their humans. We were even happier when we discovered that Perdita was expecting puppies.

When the big day came and I saw those fifteen little white balls of fluff, I was the proudest father in town!

Unfortunately Cruella de Vil had to burst in and shatter our peace.

"I heard that Perdita and Pongo have fifteen puppies," Cruella said, pulling out a chequebook and pen. "How much do you want for all of them?"

Anita tried to be polite. After all, she had known Cruella at school. But no matter how much money Cruella offered, Roger was firm. "The puppies are not for sale!" he said.

Cruella was so angry that she stormed out of the house, shouting threats. I had the feeling she meant trouble.

Over the next few weeks, the puppies grew quickly. They were such fun!

They loved to watch television. Their hero was a dog called Thunderbolt. Sometimes, they barked and growled when the bad guys appeared on the screen.

One evening, Perdita and I went out for a stroll with Roger and Anita. We left the puppies at home with Nanny. She was the one who looked after us all.

Nanny had just put the puppies to bed when the doorbell rang. It was two shady-looking men who said they worked for the electricity company. Nanny was suspicious, and wouldn't let them in. But they pushed their way past her.

"Where do you think you're going?" she cried.

Nanny tried her best, but she couldn't stop them.

Soon they found what they were after – the puppies.

**W**hen we got home, the puppies' basket was empty.

Roger called the police right way. "Our fifteen Dalmatian puppies have been stolen," he told them. "I don't know who could have done this. But please, you must find them for us."

Perdita and I were not about to wait for the police to solve the kidnapping. We decided to take matters into our own hands.

The next evening, I used the Twilight Bark to send out word of the kidnapping. What a racket! I'm sure no one in the city got much sleep that night.

But it worked. The dogs in the city were the first to hear the news. They barked the message to Towser the bloodhound and Lucy the goose, who lived out in the country.

"What is it? What's all the gossip?" asked Lucy.

"Fifteen puppies stolen!" answered Towser. "We'd best send the word along. It will be up to me to reach the Colonel!"

Then Towser began to bark with all his might, passing the message on to the Colonel, an old English sheepdog.

The Colonel and his friend Tibs the cat set to work immediately.

"I've just remembered," Tibs told the Colonel. "Two nights past, I heard puppies barking at the old de Vil mansion."

"That place has been empty for years. Something fishy is going on over there," the Colonel said. "Let's go and have a look."

Sure enough, there were signs of activity at the old mansion, so the Colonel sent Tibs to get a closer look.

What a scene! Two tough-looking men named Horace and Jasper were watching television. And all around them were spotted puppies!

Tibs crept closer to one of the puppies.

"Are you one of the fifteen stolen puppies?" Tibs whispered.

"There's ninety-nine of us altogether," answered the pup.

Meanwhile, the Colonel had passed on the news that the puppies had been found.

Of course, upon learning this, Perdita and I raced to rescue our pups.

Tibs knew there was no time to waste when he overheard Cruella de Vil arrive at the house and begin talking to Horace and Jasper. She was planning to make spotted coats out of the puppies!

"I've got no time to argue!" she shouted. "I want the job on those puppies to be done tonight!"

"We'll get on with it – as soon as the show's over," Jasper said to Horace after Cruella had left.

"Quick!" Tibs whispered to the puppies. "Follow me and don't make a sound! You're in danger. I've got to get you out of here now!"

The puppies were frightened, but they did as they were told.

Tibs led the puppies to a hole in the living room wall. Then, just as he was pushing the last pup through, Horace and Jasper noticed the dogs were missing.

Jasper grabbed a fireplace poker, and Horace picked up a broken chair leg to use as a club. Then they started searching every corner of the old mansion.

Quickly, Tibs hid the puppies under the staircase. "Shush!" the cat whispered.

But just then, the flashlight's beam lit up their hiding place!

Perdita and I had barely arrived outside the mansion when we heard Horace and Jasper shouting.

"Hurry! Something's going on in there!" I said.

We burst through the window, growling, and quickly went to work saving our puppies.

I latched onto Jasper's leg, and soon had him on the floor while Perdita made short work of Horace.

In the meantime, Tibs had managed to get the puppies safely out of the mansion. The Colonel was waiting for them outside, and led them to safety at his farm.

Soon Perdita and I were reunited with the puppies. We planned to rest at the Colonel's farm for the night. But when Horace and Jasper arrived, we all had to move on.

The weather was getting much worse, and it was hard for the puppies to walk in the deep snow.

Fortunately, we continued to get help from our friends. A collie who lived on a farm in the area came out to meet us.

"We'd just about lost hope," he said. "We have shelter for you at the dairy farm across the road. You can all rest and get an early start in the morning."

"Thank goodness!" I said.

Three cows watched as Perdita led the puppies into the barn.

"Oh, the poor little dears," said Princess. "They're completely worn out and half frozen."

"Mother, I'm hungry," one of the puppies said.

"Do you like warm milk?" Princess asked.

"Come and get it, kids," said Queenie. "It's on the house!"

The puppies lapped up all the milk they could drink, and then settled down to sleep. But the next day at dawn, we were on the run again.

A Labrador retriever was waiting for us in the next village. He gave us shelter and explained that he had arranged a lift home for us in the back of a van.

Just then, we spotted Cruella de Vil cruising through the village in her car. Nearby, Horace and Jasper were searching for us on foot.

"Oh, Pongo," Perdita said, "how will we get into the van without her seeing us?"

Then I had an idea. "We'll all roll in soot," I said. "She's looking for Dalmatians, not Labradors!"

Soon we were all black from head to tail.

Perdita and the Labrador led the first batch of puppies straight past Horace and Jasper, and into the waiting van.

"Look, Jasper," Horace remarked as the puppies trotted past him. "Do you suppose those dogs have disguised themselves?"

"You idiot!" Jasper laughed. "Dogs don't paint themselves black!"

"Those dogs are somewhere in this village," Cruella yelled to Horace and Jasper. "Now go and find them!"

The final batch of puppies had almost made it to the van when....

SPLAAT! Drops of melting snow fell on the puppies. Small white spots began to appear on their backs. Cruella looked more closely. Her brain started ticking. White spots on black dogs... of course!

"After them! After them!" she screamed.

We all made a run for it. Then, just as I lifted the last puppy safely into the van, the engine roared to life, and we were all on our way to London.

"I'll catch up with them yet!" Cruella said, stepping on the accelerator.

Cruella raced after the van, and rammed into it. She was trying to force us off the road!

We cringed in fear, wishing our driver could go faster.

Then I saw the blue truck driven by Horace and Jasper. They had taken a short cut.

Now they were barrelling down the hill, trying to cut off our van. But instead, they smashed into Cruella's car.

BAANNG! CRAASSHH! Cruella, Horace and Jasper went flying through the air, and landed in a pile of snow. They would not be able to cause any more trouble.

A little later, at the house in London, Nanny heard faint barking. The barks got louder. Suddenly the kitchen door burst open, and a pack of black dogs scampered in.

One of the big dogs jumped on Anita's lap, and tried to lick her face.

"Why, it's Perdy!" Anita cried. "And all the puppies!"

Then she looked again. "There must be a hundred of them!" she said in amazement.

"One hundred and one," said Roger, counting. "Including Perdita and Pongo. What a family!"

Everyone was delighted – even Nanny, who had quite a job on her hands trying to get us all cleaned up.

40

"What will we do with them all?" asked Anita.

"We'll keep 'em," said Roger. "We'll buy a big place in the country and live there. It'll be a plantation. A Dalmatian plantation!"

Roger was so pleased that he sat right down at the piano to write a song. And we all gathered around him, just happy to be home.

Once upon a time in a faraway land, a young prince lived in a shining castle. Although he had everything his heart desired, he was selfish and unkind.

One winter's night, an enchantress came to the castle disguised as an old beggar woman. She offered him a single rose in return for shelter from the cold. But the prince sneered at her gift, and turned her away.

So the enchantress transformed him into a hideous beast, and transformed all his servants into household objects. The spell would be broken only if the Beast could learn to love, and earned someone's love in return before the last petal fell from the enchanted rose.

Ashamed of his ugliness, the Beast locked himself away in his castle. An enchanted mirror was his only window to the outside world.

As the years passed, he lost all hope. For who could ever love a beast?

Not far from the castle, in a small village, lived a beautiful girl named Belle.

Belle loved to read tales of far-off places, magic spells and princes in disguise. She yearned for excitement in her life – and for someone with whom to share it.

That someone was definitely not the handsome Gaston, who had announced his intention to marry Belle because she was the most beautiful girl in the village. Belle considered Gaston self-centred and arrogant. Besides, she had other plans.

Belle's father, Maurice, was an inventor, although most of his inventions failed. "I'm about ready to give up on this contraption," Maurice said one day, kicking his latest project.

"You always say that," Belle laughed. "But I just know you'll win first prize at the fair."

With Belle's encouragement, Maurice finally finished one of his inventions. That afternoon, he packed it onto the wagon behind his horse, Phillipe, and headed for the fair.

Hours later, they were still on the road. "We'll have to take a short cut through the woods," Maurice decided.

The forest road was dark and scary. Then Phillipe heard wolves howling, and reared in alarm.

"Whoa, Phillipe, whoa!" Maurice cried. But the terrified horse bolted, and threw his rider off.

Maurice had to flee from the wolves on foot. Just when he felt his strength would give out, he stumbled through the rusty gates of a gloomy castle.

No one answered his knock, so Maurice stepped cautiously inside the door. "Hello?" he called.

"Shh! Not a word," a mantel clock whispered to a golden candlestick.

"Oh, Cogsworth, have a heart," the candlestick replied. Then he called out, "You are welcome here, monsieur."

Maurice was astonished to see a talking candlestick. But when Lumiere invited him to warm himself by the fire, he sank gratefully into a giant chair.

By the time Mrs. Potts arrived with her son, Chip, to offer Maurice a nice cup of tea, he was quite enjoying himself. "What service!" he said.

Just then, however, the door burst open, and the Beast's shadow fell over the room. "What are you doing here?" he growled.

The next thing Maurice knew, great claws had grabbed him and hauled him off to a barred cell in the dungeon.

Back in the village, Belle was waiting for her father to return when Gaston swaggered in with a proposal.

"Picture this," he said. "A hunting lodge, my latest kill roasting on the fire, and my little wife massaging my feet. And do you know who that little wife will be? You, Belle!"

Belle couldn't think what to say. Finally, she replied, "I'm very sorry, Gaston, but I just don't deserve you."

As she manoeuvred to get away from him, Gaston fell out the doorway and into a mud puddle – right in front of all the villagers he had invited to see his wedding. "I'll have Belle as my wife," he fumed. "Make no mistake about that."

But Belle didn't hear him, for at that moment, Phillipe galloped into the yard.

"Where's Papa?" Belle cried. "You have to take me to him!"

The tired horse carried Belle back through the woods. When she saw her father's hat on the ground inside the gate, she knew she had to enter the forbidding castle.

Lumiere took one look at Belle, and realised she was the one they had all been waiting for – the one who would break the spell. So he led the girl to her father.

"Oh, Papa! We have to get you out of here!" Belle cried. But just then, the Beast entered.

"Please let my father out. He's sick," Belle begged.

"He shouldn't have trespassed," the Beast replied. "There's nothing you can do. He's my prisoner."

"Take me, instead," Belle said.

"Then you must promise to stay here forever," the Beast replied.

So it was agreed. The Beast dragged Maurice out the door to an enchanted carriage, and sent him home.

Belle was heartbroken as she watched her father leave. She had not even been allowed to say good-bye. But she knew she had to keep her promise to the Beast.

Then the wardrobe in her bedroom told her the Beast wasn't as bad as he appeared. And the food at the castle was delicious. So Belle tried to make the best of things.

Meanwhile, as soon as he returned to their village, Maurice burst into the tavern shouting, "Help! He's got Belle locked in a dungeon!" But when he spoke of "a horrible beast," the villagers decided the old inventor was crazy.

While the others laughed at Maurice, Gaston took his friend Lefou aside. "I have a plan," he said. He had thought of a way to try to force Belle to marry him.

At the castle, Belle was not locked up at all. The Beast had given her permission to go anywhere in the castle she wanted to... except the West Wing.

Soon, the West Wing was all Belle could think about. So when no one was looking, she crept in. She found a dirty room full of cracked mirrors and broken furniture. The only beautiful, living thing was the enchanted rose, glowing inside a bell jar. She was about to touch it when the Beast roared at her.

"Why did you come here?" he bellowed. "Get out!"

Belle was terrified. Lumiere and Cogsworth saw her as she ran through the halls, but they could not stop her. She ran out the front door, saddled Phillipe and escaped into the freezing night.

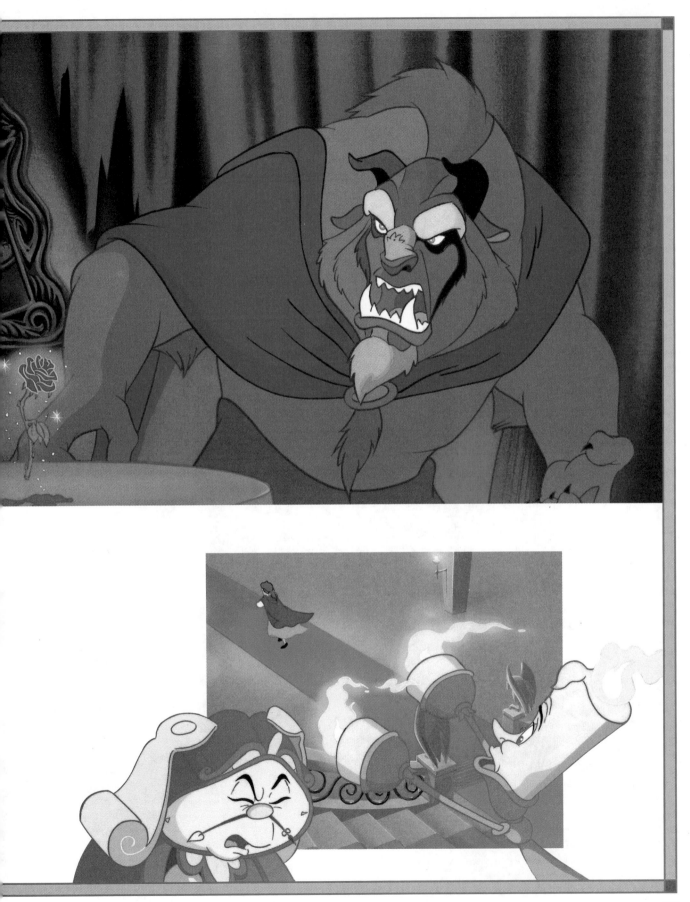

As Belle and Phillipe raced through the woods, they glimpsed the wild yellow eyes of wolves in the darkness. But when they tried to run faster, Phillipe's reins caught on a tree branch. He reared up in fear, and Belle was thrown to the ground. Instantly, snarling wolves surrounded her.

Suddenly, the Beast's giant paw snatched one of the wolves and tossed him through the air. After a fierce battle, the wolves fled whining into the forest. But the Beast had been hurt.

Belle was about to jump back on the horse when she noticed that the Beast had collapsed in pain. She hesitated only a moment before running to his side.

Belle helped the Beast back to the enchanted castle, and nursed his wounds until he was better. Before long, Belle and the Beast were reading books, eating meals, and taking walks together.

"Isn't it wonderful!" the enchanted objects agreed as they watched the couple becoming friends.

Finally, the Beast allowed the enchanted objects to dress him in new clothes.

"Tonight, when the moment is right, you must confess your love to her," Lumiere advised the Beast.

So that night, after dinner, the Beast led Belle into the ballroom and they danced together to a beautiful love song.

"Belle, are you happy here with me?" the Beast asked.

"Yes, but..." Belle said, "if only I could see my father, just for a moment."

"There is a way," the Beast told her. And then he brought out his enchanted mirror.

When Belle looked into the mirror, she saw her father lost and shivering in the woods, searching for her. "Oh, no! He's sick! He may be dying!" Belle said.

"Then you must go to him," the Beast said. "I release you. But take the mirror with you, so you will always have a way to look back... and remember me."

"How can you let her go?" Cogsworth asked, near to tears.

"Because I love her," the Beast replied.

With the mirror's help, Belle found her father and took him home. "How did you escape from that horrible beast?" her father asked.

"I didn't escape, Papa. He let me go," Belle said. "He's changed somehow."

Meanwhile, Gaston had convinced the director of the insane asylum to lock up Maurice. His plan was simple – he would convince Belle that he was the only one who could save her father – but only if she agreed to marry him.

"Everyone knows her father is a lunatic, talking about some giant beast. But Belle will do anything to protect him," Gaston explained.

But when Gaston and the director arrived, followed by a crowd of curious villagers, Belle held up the enchanted mirror, and showed them the image of the Beast. "My father's not crazy!" she protested. "The Beast is real, but he's also quite kind."

Gaston realised that Belle had feelings for the Beast instead of himself. Enraged, he snatched the mirror from her.

"She's as crazy as her old man!" he told the crowd. "The Beast will make off with your children. I say we kill him!"

And so the angry crowd followed Gaston through the woods to storm the Beast's castle.

The enchanted household objects saw the mob from the castle windows, and prepared their defence. By the time the villagers battered through the castle door, an army of angry objects was ready for them.

"Now!" Lumiere yelled, leading the attack. Immediately, forks and brooms and furniture and objects of every description hurled themselves through the air towards the astonished townspeople.

But the Beast, sure he had lost Belle forever, had no heart for fighting. "What shall we do, master?" Mrs. Potts asked him.

"It doesn't matter now. Let them come," the Beast replied. So when Gaston stormed into his room, the Beast didn't even attempt to defend himself.

When Belle arrived seconds later, she saw that Gaston had forced the Beast to the edge of the castle roof.

"No!" Belle screamed.

The sound of Belle's voice snapped the Beast into action. He grabbed Gaston by the neck and dangled him over the edge of the roof.

"Let me go! I'll do anything!" Gaston pleaded.

Full of rage, the Beast hesitated for just a moment. Then he realised he was not really a beast at heart. He tossed Gaston safely back on the balcony, and turned towards Belle, who had raced up the stairs to find him.

But just as the Beast moved to embrace Belle, Gaston pulled a long hunting knife from his boot...

...and stabbed the Beast in the back.

The Beast let out a howl of pain. Gaston took a frightened step backwards, tripped over the edge, and plunged from the roof.

But the Beast had been terribly wounded. Belle ran to his side and embraced him. "You came back," the Beast whispered. "At least I got to see you one last time."

"Don't talk like that. You'll be all right," Belle said, fighting back tears.

In the Beast's room, the last petal was about to drop from the rose.

"No! Please don't leave me. I love you," Belle sobbed, leaning down to kiss him just as the last petal fell.

Magically, the Beast rose, and changed back into his human form.

"Belle, it's me," said the Prince.

Belle rushed into the Prince's arms. As they kissed, magic filled the air. Soon Lumiere, Cogsworth, Mrs. Potts and Chip, and all the other enchanted objects were transformed back into their human forms.

That night, the castle was filled with love as Belle and the Prince danced and danced, barely able to take their eyes off each other. And the castle was once again filled with life and laughter.

It was that special time of year. All around the world, in forests, fields and barnyards, the stork was delivering babies of various shapes and sizes to their new animal mothers.

Mrs. Jumbo, the elephant, searched the sky anxiously. Would she be one of the lucky ones to get a new baby? But all the storks passed by, and still there was no bundle for Mrs. Jumbo.

"Now I'll have to wait until next year." Mrs. Jumbo sighed as she shuffled aboard the circus train the following morning. It was time for the circus to move to another town.

SHOW ON EARTH

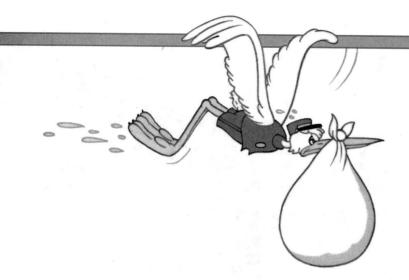

The train was steaming across the countryside when the stork finally caught up with Mrs. Jumbo.

"Here is a baby with eyes of blue, straight from heaven, right to you. Sign here, please," the stork said.

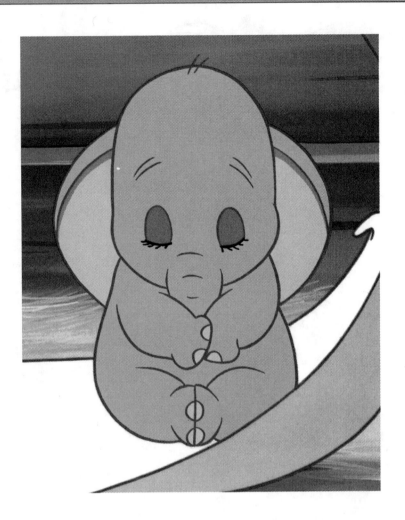

Mrs. Jumbo started to untie the package. "Do hurry, dear," urged an elephant in a neighbouring stall. "I'm on pins and needles."

Finally, Mrs. Jumbo got the knot open. There, sitting straight and still, was a baby elephant, his eyes still closed.

"Oooooh!" the other elephants chorused. "Isn't he a darling?"

One of the elephants stretched out her trunk to tickle the baby under his chin. "Kootchy, kootchy, kootchy," she said.

The baby wrinkled his trunk. Then he sneezed a sneeze so powerful that his two enormous ears flapped out to the sides.

The other elephants rocked back on their heels in shock.

"Isn't there some mistake?" asked one.

"Just look at those ears!" said another.

They all agreed on one thing. The ears were extremely funny. In fact, one said, the baby looked so ridiculous that he should be called Dumbo. "Dumbo! That's good," they all agreed.

Mrs. Jumbo turned away from them, and hugged her baby tightly.

At the next town, the animals marched in a parade to announce the arrival of the circus. Little Dumbo walked proudly behind his mother, carrying a doll on his back.

Then it was time for the show. "Step right up and get your tickets!" the circus barker cried.

A group of boys in the queue for tickets noticed Dumbo eating his supper next to his mother. One nasty boy started teasing Dumbo, and pulling at his ears. "Isn't that the funniest thing you ever saw?" the boy jeered.

Mrs. Jumbo did her best to protect her baby. But when the boy started to hurt Dumbo by pulling on his ears, she lost her patience. She spanked the boy with her trunk, just hard enough to scare him.

"Hey! Stop that! You're hurting me!" the boy shouted. "Help! Murder!"

His cries brought the Ringmaster, who wrongly thought Mrs. Jumbo had attacked the boy. "Tie her down!" he shouted.

The Ringmaster snapped a whip in Mrs. Jumbo's face, and she reared in fright, fighting against her ropes.

Convinced she had gone mad, the Ringmaster had her locked up.

The other elephants blamed Dumbo for the whole situation. "Him with those ears that only a mother could love," one said. So instead of helping him find his mother, they gave him the cold shoulder.

Luckily, Timothy Q. Mouse noticed the lonely little elephant, and decided to befriend him. To cheer Dumbo up, the mouse said, "You know, lots of people with big ears are famous. All we've got to do is build an act!"

That night, Timothy climbed onto the Ringmaster's pillow, and whispered his idea into the sleeping man's ear. Dumbo, the baby elephant, would bounce from a springboard to the top of a giant pyramid built of elephants!

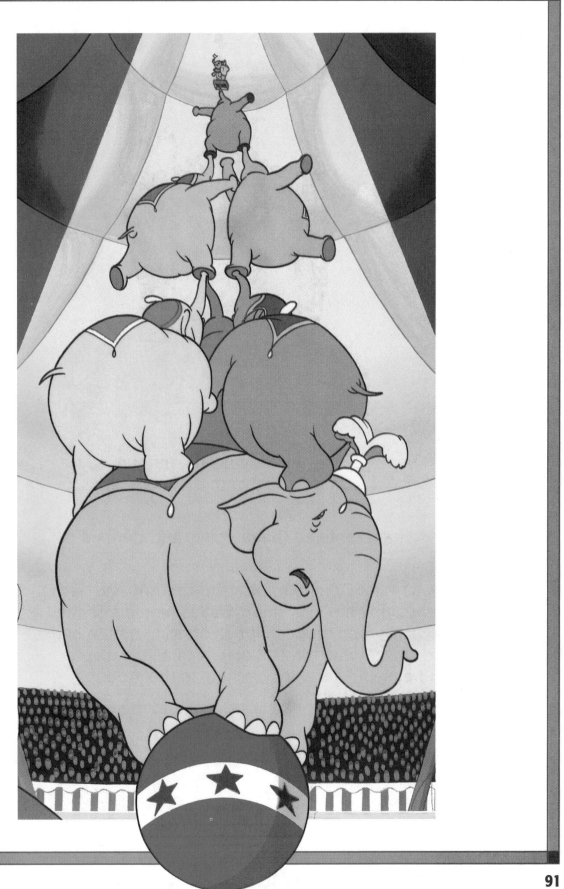

At the next performance, the Ringmaster announced his new act with great fanfare, promising "a pyramid of ponderous, pulsating, pulchritudinous pachyderms!"

The adult elephants entered the ring first, and climbed one by one onto a large ball.

Then it was time for Dumbo's entrance. Timothy had tied back his ears so he wouldn't trip over them. But as he ran into the ring, the knot came undone. Dumbo tripped and went flying off the end of the springboard straight into the ball on which all the elephants were balancing. The elephants went crashing to the ground.

Within seconds, the crowd had scattered, and the circus tent lay in ruins.

The Ringmaster was not too pleased with the little elephant, but he had to find some use for Dumbo, so...

Dumbo became a clown. He had to wear baby clothes, and jump out of a fake burning building into a tub of sticky cream. When the crowd laughed, it made Dumbo feel like crying.

But again, Timothy found a way to cheer up Dumbo. He took him to see his mother.

Mrs. Jumbo reached her trunk through the bars of her cage, and cradled her baby.

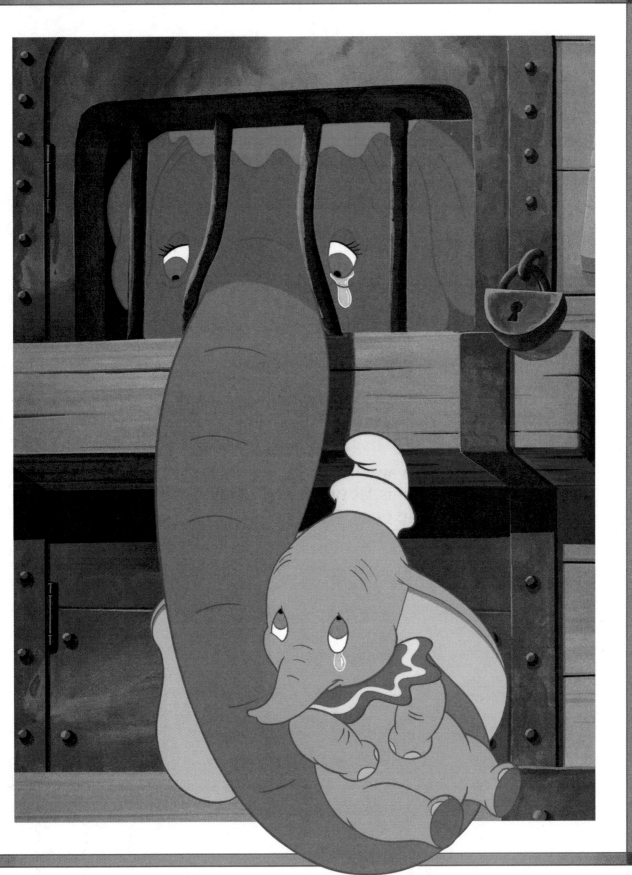

Dumbo could not stay long with his mother. He had to go back to the circus. On the way, he was crying so hard that he got the hiccups.

"Nothing a little water won't cure," Timothy said, and he led Dumbo to a large wooden tub in the corner of the tent. "Here. Take a trunkful!" he said.

Soon Dumbo fell asleep and dreamed of pink elephants, as well as green ones and white ones. And Dumbo had the weird sensation that he was flying!

The next morning, a group of crows found Dumbo and Timothy sleeping high in a tree.

"They aren't dead, are they?" one of the crows asked.

"No. Dead people don't snore," his mate said.

After further debate, the crows decided to wake the sleeping pair.

As soon as Dumbo realised he was in a tree, he toppled off the branch, and into the pond below.

As Timothy shook himself dry, he started wondering exactly how they had got up into the tree. They couldn't have climbed, or jumped...

"Maybe you flew up," one of the crows jeered.

"That's it!" Timothy cried. "Dumbo! You flew!"

Now all they had to do was test the theory. Dumbo was reluctant, until the crows came up with a magic feather for him to hold.

"Now you can fly!" Timothy said.

Dumbo stood nervously, holding the magic feather firmly with his trunk. He closed his eyes.

The crows gave Dumbo a shove, shouting "Heave ho — off you go!" Dumbo flapped his ears.

At first, Timothy could not see through the great clouds of dust that had been raised by Dumbo's ears. But then he spotted Dumbo's shadow on the ground below. "Hot diggity! You're flying!" he shouted.

Dumbo opened his eyes. It was true! He was flying!

"Now I've seen everything," one of the crows chortled. "Those city folks are really in for a surprise!"

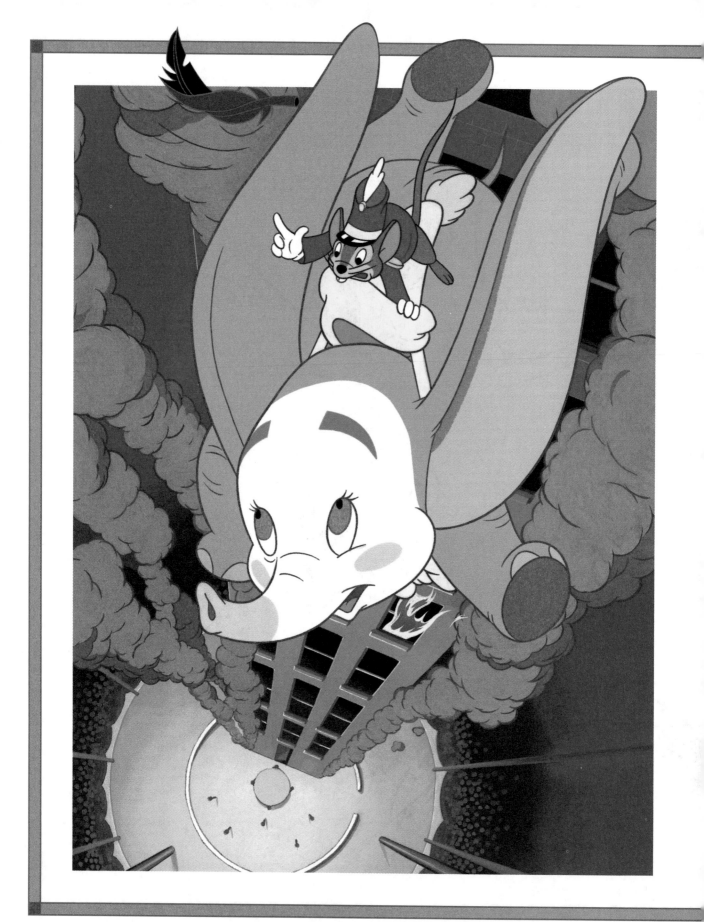

That night, Dumbo had to jump again out of the burning building. "Come on, jump," the clown fireman shouted as he held one side of the net far below.

This time, Dumbo was not afraid. He had his magic feather. "Are they in for a surprise!" Timothy said.

But as Dumbo began to fly, the wind pulled the feather from his grasp. He froze in terror. "Come on, fly!" Timothy urged. "The magic feather was just a joke! You can fly. Honestly you can!"

Finally, Dumbo flapped his ears. Down below, the clowns gaped in amazement. The little elephant could fly!

Dumbo became an overnight sensation. Everywhere the circus went, people came to see Dumbo the Flying Elephant.

He performed nose dives and spins and loops — and Mrs. Jumbo watched proudly from her place of honour.

"You're making history!" Timothy said.

Indeed, Dumbo was the star of the circus. But he was just happy to be with his mama again.

Hi, there! I'm Jiminy Cricket, and I want to tell you a little story about dreams coming true. Now, maybe you don't believe that dreams and wishes can come true. I didn't either, but let me tell you what made me change my mind.

You see, I wander from hearth to hearth, singing, and one night my travels took me to a sleepy little town. I noticed a cosy house that belonged to an old woodcarver named Geppetto, and decided to stay there for the night.

You never saw such a place! Full of clocks and music boxes and wooden toys. Geppetto was putting the finishing touches on a wooden puppet.

"Now, I have just the name for you," Geppetto said when he finished. "Pinocchio!"

Geppetto was so pleased with his new creation that he danced around the room with Pinocchio, introducing him to Figaro the cat and Cleo the goldfish.

Later that night, just before he went to sleep, Geppetto looked out at the night sky. "Oh, Figaro, look! The wishing star!" he said.

> *Star light, star bright,*
> *First star I see tonight,*
> *I wish I may,*
> *I wish I might,*
> *Have the wish I make tonight!*

"Figaro, you know what I wished?" Geppetto asked. The cat shook his head. "I wished that my little Pinocchio might be a *real* boy," Geppetto said.

Soon, everyone except me was fast asleep. And so I was the only one to see the Blue Fairy arrive to grant Geppetto's wish.

The fairy pointed her wand at Pinocchio, and recited a spell. Pinocchio turned his head. "I can move!" he said. "I can talk!"

"Yes," the Blue Fairy said. "I have given you life."

"Am I a real boy?" Pinocchio asked.

"Not yet," the fairy explained. "But prove yourself brave, truthful and unselfish, and someday you will be a real boy."

The fairy explained that Pinocchio would also have to learn to choose between right and wrong. And she appointed me to be his conscience. *Sir* Jiminy Cricket, she called me!

Then she gave Pinocchio one last piece of advice. "Be a good boy, and always let your conscience be your guide," she said.

After she had left, I tried to explain to Pinocchio how to follow the straight and narrow path. "And anytime you need me, just whistle," I told him.

Of course, then I had to teach him how to whistle, and we woke up Geppetto. Wasn't he surprised!

"My wish! It's come true!" he cried. "This calls for a celebration!"

But soon Geppetto realised how late it was and told Pinocchio it was time for bed. "Tomorrow, you've got to go to school," he said.

"Why?" asked Pinocchio.

"To learn things and become clever," Geppetto replied.

Bright and early the next morning Pinocchio was on his way to school, like a good boy, when he ran into two scoundrels, Honest John and Gideon. They tripped him with a cane, and then they convinced him to forget about school.

"Take the easy road to success," Honest John said. "Acting!"

I had slept in. My first day on the job, too! So by the time I caught up with Pinocchio, he was on his way to the theatre.

Honest John and Gideon led Pinocchio to a man named Stromboli, who owned a puppet show.

"The only marionette who can sing and dance absolutely without the aid of strings!" Stromboli announced later as Pinocchio made his first appearance on stage.

Pinocchio danced with a number of real marionettes wearing costumes. The crowd loved him.

"You are sensational!" Stromboli told Pinocchio. "I will push you in the public eye. Your face, she will be on everybody's tongue."

"Will she?" Pinocchio asked.

"Yes!" Stromboli said.

Pinocchio was delighted with his success. But when he announced that he was going home to tell his father about his new job, Stromboli laughed. "Oh, that is very comical!" he chuckled.

Then he tossed Pinocchio into a cage and slammed the door shut. "This will be your home, where I can find you always!" he said. "You will make lots of money for me, and when you grow too old, you will make good firewood!"

That night, alone in the dark, Pinocchio called my name. "Jiminy! Oh, Jiminy," he called. Then he remembered he had to whistle if he needed me.

"What did he do to you?" I cried when I saw him swinging in the cage.

"Oh, he was angry. He said he was going to push my face in everybody's eye!" Pinocchio wailed.

"Don't worry, son. I'll have you out of there in no time," I promised. But I could not open the lock.

We had almost given up hope when the Blue Fairy appeared again. "Pinocchio," she said, "why didn't you go to school?"

"I was going to school 'til I met somebody," Pinocchio said, starting off truthfully. But then he told a fantastic tale about meeting two big monsters, with big green eyes, who had tied him in a sack, and chopped him into firewood.

With each new lie, Pinocchio's nose grew longer, until it was as long as the branch of a tree. "My nose! What's happened!" he cried.

"Perhaps you haven't been telling the truth," the fairy said. "You see, Pinocchio, a lie keeps growing until it's as plain as the nose on your face."

So Pinocchio promised never to lie again, and the fairy agreed to set him free. "But this is the last time I can help you," she said.

Our way home took us past an inn, where Honest John and Gideon were talking to the Coachman.

"Would you fellows like to make some real money?" the Coachman asked.

The Coachman told them he was collecting stupid and disobedient boys, so he could take them to a place called Pleasure Island. "Any good prospects you find, bring 'em to me," he said.

As soon as Honest John and Gideon stepped outside, they spotted Pinocchio. Pinocchio was determined to be good, but he stopped to tell them what had happened to his acting job.

"You poor, poor boy. You must be a nervous wreck," Honest John said. "There's only one cure. A holiday on Pleasure Island!"

"But I can't go," Pinocchio said.

"Of course you can," said Honest John, grabbing hold of Pinocchio's arm.

Honest John filled Pinocchio's head with promises of fun and games on the island. So by the time Pinocchio climbed onto the coach, already full of boys, he was looking forward to his holiday, and had forgotten all his promises.

He quickly made friends with a boy named Lampwick, who told him even more delightful stories about Pleasure Island.

"No school," Lampwick said. "Plenty to eat. Plenty to drink. And it's all free!"

It sounded so exciting that Pinocchio barely noticed the unhappy faces on the donkeys pulling the coach.

The Coachman delivered the boys to a boat, which carried them across the water to an island amusement park. As the boat unloaded, a voice was shouting, "Hurry, hurry. Get your cake, pie and ice cream. Eat all you can. Stuff yourselves. Hurry! Hurry!"

As the boys rushed towards the voice, they did not see the Coachman smiling evilly behind them.

Pinocchio and Lampwick ate their fill, then stopped in a pool hall for a game.

Pinocchio noticed there was no one else around. "Where do you think all the kids went to, Lampwick?" he said.

"What do you care? You're having a good time, aren't you?" Lampwick replied. "This is the life!"

"Yes," said Pinocchio.

That's when I caught up with him. "How do you ever expect to be a real boy!" I said. "Look at yourself! You're coming right home with me!"

"Who's the beetle?" Lampwick asked, picking me up.

Pinocchio explained that I was his conscience. "He tells me what's right and wrong," he said.

But in the end, Pinocchio decided to ignore me, and stay with his new friend, Lampwick. So I decided to go home without him.

But when I reached the boat dock, I saw a strange scene. The Coachman was loading a group of donkeys onto the boat. Some of them were wearing hats and clothes that looked familiar. Then I worked it out — the Coachman had been changing all the boys into donkeys!

When I realised what was going on, I knew I had to warn Pinocchio. Then I heard him calling my name.

I rushed back into the pool hall.

I was too late. Lampwick had already turned into a donkey. And Pinocchio had grown long ears and a tail.

"Come on!" I cried to Pinocchio. "Before you get any worse."

We raced across the island, trying to stay out of the Coachman's sight. We had to climb over some rocks to get to the edge of the island. Then we found ourselves on a cliff overlooking the sea.

It was a long way down.

"Hurry up, before they see us," I said. "You've got to jump!"

It was a long swim, but we finally made it to dry land. "Come on, let's go home," I said.

Pinocchio ran to the door of Geppetto's house shouting, "Father! Father! I'm home!" But no one answered.

So we looked through the window. The house was empty. And Geppetto's work bench was covered with cobwebs. "He's gone!" Pinocchio said.

We were sitting on the steps, trying to decide what to do, when a piece of paper fluttered down from the sky.

"It's a message about your father!" I said.

"Where is he?" Pinocchio asked.

"It says here, he went looking for you and he was swallowed by a whale name Monstro," I read.

Pinocchio looked heartbroken.

"But wait!" I said. "He's alive! Inside the whale at the bottom of the sea."

"I'm going to find him," Pinocchio said as he headed off.

"Are you mad?" I asked. "He's in a whale!"

But Pinocchio kept going until he reached the coast. I watched him tie his donkey tail around a big rock, to stop him from floating.

"This whale, Monstro, he swallows whole ships alive," I warned.

"Good-bye, Jiminy," Pinocchio said as he prepared to jump in.

Well, I couldn't let him go alone, could I?

"Wow! What a big place," Pinocchio said when we reached the bottom.

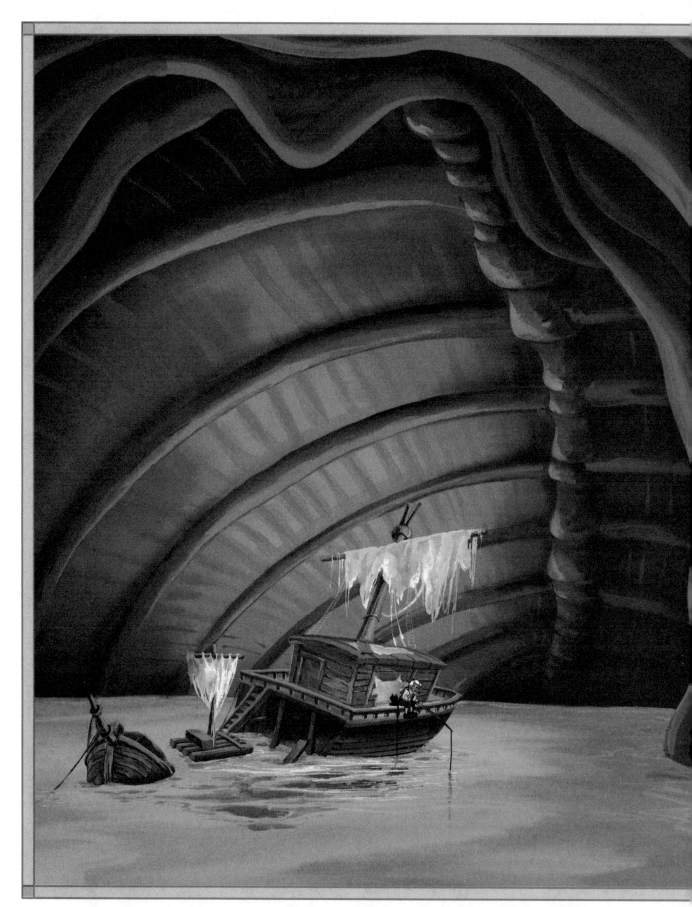

Pinocchio asked a number of fish if they knew the whereabouts of Monstro the Whale. But when they heard Monstro's name, they swam away.

We had no way of knowing that Monstro was sleeping on the ocean floor nearby.

Inside his huge belly, Geppetto and Figaro were sitting on the deck of their ruined boat, fishing.

"Not a bite for days. We can't hold out much longer," Geppetto said. He knew that if the whale did not wake up and swallow some fish soon, they would starve. "I never thought it would end this way," he said sadly.

At that moment, a school of fish swam so close to Monstro that they nearly collided with him. The commotion woke the whale, and he gave chase.

Seconds later, he opened his huge jaw and swallowed hundreds of them. Pinocchio was in the same mouthful of water. I was left behind.

"Here they come! Tuna!" Geppetto shouted. "We will eat!"

He started scooping tuna into the boat. "Enough for weeks," he said gleefully. Geppetto was hauling in fish so fast that at first, he didn't notice Pinocchio holding tightly to a tuna.

When he finally saw him, he was dumbfounded. "Pinocchio!" Geppetto cried.

"Father!" Pinocchio yelled, leaping into Geppetto's arms.

They were all together again — Pinocchio, Geppetto, Figaro, and Cleo. But Pinocchio was anxious to find a way out of the whale.

"I came to save you!" he announced.

"Oh, no, son. I've tried every way," Geppetto said. "I've even built a raft."

"That's it!" Pinocchio said. "We'll take the raft, and when the whale opens his mouth..."

"It's hopeless," Geppetto said. "He only opens his mouth when he's eating. Then everything comes in, nothing goes out! Let's make a nice fire, cook some fish..."

"A fire! That's it!" Pinocchio cried.

He built a fire using barrels, chairs, and anything that would burn. "We'll make him sneeze," he explained.

I was still floating around near the whale's mouth when suddenly the whale sneezed, and the raft came whizzing past my head!

"Wait for me!" I shouted.

Pinocchio and Geppetto paddled desperately to get as far as possible from the whale. But the fire and smoke had made the whale furious! He charged at them.

"He's trying to catch us! Paddle, son!" Geppetto shouted.

Then the whale's great tail crashed down on the raft, smashing it to bits.

Pinocchio bobbed to the surface. "Father!" he called, looking around.

Nearby, Geppetto was hanging onto a piece of debris from the raft. He was sinking fast. "Pinocchio, swim for shore," he shouted weakly. "Save yourself!"

But Pinocchio swam towards Geppetto. He grabbed his collar just before Geppetto sank beneath the waves, and towed him towards shore.

I rode the waves on an empty bottle to get to the shore. Geppetto was already there, on the beach, barely regaining consciousness. Figaro and Cleo had been washed safely to shore beside him.

Where was Pinocchio? I climbed a rock and called his name. Geppetto and I saw him at the same time, lying motionless between the rocks, face down in the surf.

Geppetto carried Pinocchio's quiet body back home, and laid him on the bed.

All night, Geppetto knelt by the side of the bed, crying.

"My boy, my brave little boy," he sobbed.

As Pinocchio slept, he heard the voice of the Blue Fairy.

*Prove yourself brave, truthful, and unselfish,*
*and some day you will be a real boy.*

Then the room where Pinocchio lay filled with light. "Awake, Pinocchio, awake," the voice said.

Pinocchio opened his eyes, and sat up. "Father, what are you crying for?" he asked.

"Because you're dead, Pinocchio," Geppetto replied.

"No, I'm not!" Pinocchio said.

"Yes, you are. Now, lie down," his father said.

"But Father, I'm alive, and — see? — I'm real," Pinocchio said. "I'm a real boy!"

"You *are* a real boy!" Geppetto said joyfully.

"Whoopee!" I shouted.

Figaro grabbed Cleo and kissed her. Geppetto started all the clocks in the house, until they began chiming. Then he wound up his music box, grabbed his accordion and played until the house was filled with the sound of bells and music.

It was a good time for me to slip away. Outside the door, I looked up at the wishing star. "Thank you," I said. "He deserved to be a real boy!"

The star twinkled. The next thing I knew, I was wearing a star-shaped badge. *Official Conscience*, it said.

I suppose we all had our dreams come true.

# THE
# LION KING

Animals came from far and wide to celebrate the birth of King Mufasa's son. When Rafiki, the wise, old mystic, stood at the edge of Pride Rock and held the infant high, all the animals bowed before Simba, their new prince.

Mufasa's brother, Scar, was the only one absent from the ceremony.

Later, Mufasa sought him out.

"Is anything wrong?" Mufasa asked his brother.

"It must have slipped my mind," Scar replied.

But the truth was, Scar was smouldering with jealousy and anger. The young Prince Simba had taken his place as next in line to be king.

When Simba was a little older, Mufasa led him one morning at dawn to the top of Pride Rock. "Everything the light touches is our kingdom," Mufasa said. Then he explained that one day, it would all belong to Simba.

"What about that shadowy place?" asked Simba, looking into the distance.

"That is beyond our borders. You must never go there," Mufasa replied soberly.

"But I thought a king can do whatever he wants," Simba said.

"There's a lot more to being king than getting your way all the time," his father replied.

Later that day, Simba's uncle Scar told him that the shadowy place was an elephant graveyard. "Only the bravest lions go there," Scar said.

Cunning Scar! He knew Simba would not be able to resist the challenge of proving how brave he was.

As Scar had hoped, Simba ran straight to his best friend, Nala.

"Come on!" he said. "I just heard about this great place!"

The two cubs soon managed to escape the watchful eyes of Zazu, who had been assigned to baby-sit them. Then they headed for the elephant graveyard.

Suddenly, the two cubs came upon an enormous, hollow-eyed skull. "This is it!" Simba announced proudly.

"Wow! It's really creepy!" Nala said.

"I know. Let's explore!" Simba replied. He was about to climb into one of the huge eye sockets when an irritated Zazu caught up with them, and ordered the cubs home.

Simba was trying to argue with Zazu, when they were interrupted by the hideous laughter of hyenas. Simba froze in his tracks.

"Well, well, well," one of the hyenas said, "what have we got here?"

Zazu suggested that it was a good time to leave.

"What's your hurry?" Shenzi said. "We'd love you to stick around for dinner."

"Yes, we could have whatever's 'lion' around. Get it?" Banzai added.

The hyenas became so absorbed in making puns that they almost let their dinner get away.

Then Shenzi noticed that the trio had managed to sneak off. "Get them!" she shouted.

The hyenas chased Simba and Nala inside the rib cage of an elephant carcass, which snapped closed on them like the bars of a jail.

Then, just as the hyenas closed in on the cubs, there was a mighty roar, and a giant paw sent the hyenas flying. "Don't you ever come near my son again!" King Mufasa commanded.

Later, Simba tried to explain his behaviour. "I was just trying to be brave – like you, Dad."

"Being brave doesn't mean you look for trouble," Mufasa said.

"But you're not scared of anything!" Simba countered.

"I was today," his father said. "I thought I might lose you."

That night, Mufasa showed Simba the evening sky. "The great kings of the past look down on us from those stars," Mufasa said. "They will always be there to guide you... and so will I."

Unfortunately, Mufasa still did not realise that his own brother Scar presented the greatest threat to Simba.

Scar was more determined than ever to get rid of Simba. And this time, he would take care of Mufasa, too. So first, he arranged for the cub to be caught in a stampede of wildebeests.

Then, once Scar was sure that Simba was in mortal danger, he yelled to Mufasa. "Quick! Stampede! Simba's down there!"

Mufasa leapt into the gorge and snatched the cub out of the path of the deadly hooves. He set Simba safely on a rocky ledge. But then the rock crumbled under Mufasa's paws, and he fell.

Mufasa was badly injured. Gathering all his strength, he tried to crawl back out of the gorge.

Scar was waiting for him on the ledge. "Brother, help me!" Mufasa begged.

But Scar let him drop into the stampeding herd.

Simba saw his father fall, although he did not know his uncle was responsible.

The cub raced into the gorge to try to wake his father. But the great Lion King was dead.

While Simba grieved, Scar suddenly appeared out of the dust. "Simba," he asked, "what have you done?"

"He tried to save me," Simba answered. "It was an accident. I didn't mean for it to..."

"Of course, you didn't. No one ever means for these things to happen," Scar said. "But the king is dead. If it weren't for you, he'd still be alive!"

"What'll I do?" Simba asked, sobbing even harder.

"Run away, Simba... run away and never return!" Scar told him.

Confused and heartbroken, Simba began to run. He did not see the hyenas join Scar, or hear his uncle order them to get rid of him once and for all.

But soon Simba realised the hyenas were following him. They chased the cub all the way to the edge of a plateau. There was only one way out. Simba leaped off the edge into a tangle of thorns.

"If you ever come back, we'll kill you!" the hyenas shouted after him.

Injured and exhausted, Simba stumbled across the hot African desert. Vultures circled above him. Finally he fainted. When he opened his eyes again, a meerkat and a warthog were standing over him. They had pulled him to an oasis and splashed water on his face.

"You okay, kid?" asked the meerkat.

"You nearly died," said the warthog.

"Where are you from?" the meerkat asked.

"Who cares?" Simba said quietly. "I can't go back."

"Then you're an outcast!" cried the meerkat. "So are we! My name's Timon, and this is Pumbaa. Take my advice, kid. You've got to put your past behind you. No past, no future, no worries — *Hakuna matata!*"

So Simba followed Timon and Pumbaa to their jungle home. Soon he adapted to their diet of bugs and grubs — as well as their easy-going lifestyle.

Time passed, and Simba grew into a young lion. He led a happy life, although when he thought about his father, he grew sad.

One day, Simba heard his friends cry for help. He found Pumbaa stuck under a tree root, while a hungry lioness approached him. Simba quickly leapt into action and pounced on her.

As the lions tussled, Timon gave Pumbaa a blow-by-blow account. "He's got her," Timon cried. "No, she's got him!"

The lioness had Simba pinned to the ground, when she suddenly paused. Simba looked into the lioness's eyes. "Nala?" he asked incredulously.

"It's me! Simba!" he added.

"Hey! What's going on here?" asked Timon in confusion.

Simba introduced everyone, but Nala could not stop staring at him. "Everyone thinks you're dead," she said.

As they strolled through the jungle, Nala told Simba how Scar had let the hyenas take over the Pride Lands, and destroy everything. Then she tried to convince Simba to return as rightful king.

But Simba insisted he could not go back. "I'm no king," he said.

"You could be!" Nala argued. But it was no use.

That night, Simba was still thinking about his decision when an old baboon appeared. It was Rafiki! He told Simba he could help him understand who he was, and what he was supposed to do.

"I know your father," Rafiki explained.

"I hate to tell you this, but my father died a long time ago," Simba replied, not recognising Rafiki as the mystic who had presented him at his birth.

"No! He's alive," the baboon said. He led Simba to a pool and pointed to Simba's reflection.

"You see?" Rafiki asked. "He lives in you!"

Then Mufasa's image appeared in the stars above Simba. "You must take your place in the Circle of Life," Mufasa gently commanded.

"But I've made a place for myself here," Simba replied. "I'm not who I used to be. How can I go back?"

"Remember who you are. You are my son and the one true king," Mufasa answered.

After that, Simba wasted no time in heading home to challenge his uncle. But as he crossed into his kingdom, he saw devastation everywhere. The great herds were gone. The grasslands were dead.

Meanwhile, at Pride Rock, the hyenas complained to Scar that the lionesses had not brought them any food for days.

"The herds have moved on," Simba's mother Sarabi explained. Their only hope was to leave Pride Rock.

"We're not going anywhere," Scar growled.

"Then you are sentencing us to death," Sarabi replied.

"So be it. I am the king and I make the rules!"

"If you were half the king Mufasa was...," Sarabi began. But the mere mention of Mufasa's name enraged Scar.

As Scar roared at Sarabi, he looked up and saw a great lion outlined against a blaze of heat lightning.

"This is my kingdom now," Simba proclaimed. "Step down, Scar!"

Instead Scar stepped toward Simba.

"Do your friends know you are responsible for your father's death?" Scar asked slyly. "You're guilty."

Then Scar backed Simba off the edge of a cliff. As Simba hung on by his claws, Scar sneered, "Now, this looks familiar. Where have I seen this before? Oh, yes... that's just the way your father looked before I killed him."

Finally knowing the truth about his father's death, Simba gathered all his strength and leapt toward his uncle.

"Help me! Help me, you idiots!" Scar yelled to his hyenas. But at that moment, Nala and the other lionesses attacked the hyenas.

Lightning had set fire to the dry savannah grasses. Scar took advantage of the smoke and the confusion of battle to sneak away.

But Simba spotted his uncle at the edge of Pride Rock, and cornered him. When Scar tried to talk his way out of a fight, Simba repeated the advice Scar had given him years before. "Run away and never return," he commanded.

In response, Scar lunged at Simba, and fell over the edge of the cliff.

As rain began to fall, Simba stood as king at the edge of Pride Rock and roared triumphantly. The lionesses roared back with joy.

Soon, under the rule of the wise and brave Simba, the Pride Lands flourished. The herds returned to graze, and food was plentiful again.

Not long afterwards, the animals gathered once more to celebrate the birth of the king's son.

Simba and Nala watched proudly as Rafiki held their new cub high over Pride Rock.

Simba remembered something his father had told him. "A king's time as ruler rises and sets like the sun. One day the sun will set on my time here and rise with you as the new ruler."

One day Simba would pass on these same words to his own cub.

It was the day that all the undersea kingdom had been awaiting. Princess Ariel, the Little Mermaid, was going to make her singing debut. Her father, King Triton, was particularly proud. Ariel had the most beautiful voice in the undersea world, according to Sebastian, the crab. Sebastian was the castle's music director.

All the guests had assembled. Sebastian had tuned up the orchestra.

Ariel's older sisters began the concert, but when a giant seashell opened to reveal the Little Mermaid, Ariel was nowhere to be found.

"Ariel!" King Triton roared.

"My concert is ruined!" Sebastian wailed.

As usual, Ariel was exploring with her friend Flounder. Ariel was fascinated with the world of humans. She loved collecting the strange objects they had dropped or lost in the sea.

Today, Ariel and Flounder were exploring a sunken ship, and found a fork.

She took it to Scuttle, the sea gull, to find out what it was. Scuttle considered himself an expert on humans.

"It's a dinglehopper," he declared. "Humans use these babies to straighten their hair."

Suddenly, Ariel remembered the concert. "Oh, my gosh!" she cried, and swam home as fast as she could.

Ariel didn't know that Ursula, the Sea Witch, was keeping an eye on all her activities. King Triton had banished Ursula from the palace long ago, and now she was plotting revenge.

As Ariel had feared, her father was furious that she had missed the concert. "You are never to have anything to do with humans again. Never!" he commanded.

But then, after Ariel had left, King Triton felt some remorse.

"Maybe she needs someone to keep an eye on her," he sighed to Sebastian.

Sebastian soon found himself with a new job — looking after Ariel. He followed her to the grotto where she kept her treasures.

"If only I could be part of the human world," the mermaid said to Flounder.

Moments later, Ariel spotted a dark shape high above. "A ship!" she cried, as she swam for the surface.

"No, Ariel!" called Sebastian. But Ariel did not look back.

Ariel had seen many ships before. But this was the first time she was able to swim close enough to see the humans on board. They were having a birthday party for someone named Prince Eric.

When darkness came, the sailors lit up the sky with fireworks. But no one, except a big sheepdog named Max, noticed Ariel.

Prince Eric received a statue of himself as a birthday gift from his friend, Sir Grimsby.

"It's really something," he said in thanks, though secretly he was embarrassed by the huge replica of himself.

Then it was time for the humans to dance! Even Max joined in!

The humans were having such a good time, and Ariel was so absorbed in the spectacle, that no one noticed the black clouds approaching.

In an instant, a great storm struck. Huge waves threatened to overturn the ship.

As lightning illuminated the sky, Ariel could see the sailors lower a lifeboat, and scramble in. Eric noticed Max was missing, and went back to search for him. Then, just as he lowered Max safely into the lifeboat, there was an explosion. Eric was tossed into the raging sea.

Ariel darted through the waves to the spot where she had seen the prince fall. Where was he? She plunged beneath the water, and spotted him sinking fast.

Ariel managed to haul the prince to the surface, and hold his head above water until she pulled him ashore.

The next morning, Scuttle saw Ariel with the unconscious Eric on the beach.

"No pulse," he announced, listening to Eric's foot.

"No, look! He's breathing," Ariel said. "Oh, he's so beautiful!"

At that moment, she knew she loved Eric. She began to sing. Eric's eyelids fluttered.

Suddenly, Ariel heard Max bark. Ariel knew that Prince Eric's friends must be looking for him.

Ariel slipped quickly back into the sea, and hid behind a nearby rock so she could watch the beach. Sure enough, seconds later, Max sniffed out his master. He was followed by Grimsby who took the prince home.

All Eric could remember later was that someone had been with him. He had no idea what she looked like, but the sound of her voice lingered in his ears.

When Ariel got home, she was delighted to find the statue of Prince Eric in her grotto. Somehow, Flounder had been able to rescue it for her. "Oh, thank you! I do so love him," Ariel sighed.

But when King Triton found out that Ariel had gone to the surface and met a human, he went straight to her grotto. "You disobeyed me!" he shouted. "I have no choice but to punish you!"

He raised his trident, and blasted Ariel's beloved treasures — including the statue — to bits.

Ursula watched the destruction from her palace, and gloated with pleasure. "I think the time is ripe," she said to Flotsam and Jetsam, her two slippery hench-eels.

Ariel was sobbing over the broken statue when Flotsam and Jetsam, following Ursula's instructions, slithered up next to her. "We know someone who can help you," Flotsam hissed.

Ariel was desperate. She followed the pair to the Sea Witch's grisly den.

Ursula oozed sympathy. "The solution to your problem is simple, my dear," she purred. "You must become a human."

"But how?" Ariel asked.

"Just sign this contract," Ursula said. "It says that I agree to make you human for three days." In return, however, Ariel would have to surrender her beautiful voice to the Sea Witch.

And there was one other small clause — "If, after three days, Prince Eric does not kiss you, you belong to me!" Ursula said.

Sebastian who had followed Ariel to the rendezvous cried out, "No, Ariel! Don't sign! Don't listen to her!"

"I must," Ariel replied. "I love Eric. This is the only way."

"Clever girl," Ursula said. Ariel signed the contract, and Ursula worked her magic.

Soon after, Ariel was above water on a beach, and Scuttle was staring at her new legs in wonder. "What's going on, Ariel?" Scuttle asked. "There's something different about you."

"Ariel's not a mermaid anymore," Sebastian explained.

Prince Eric had been searching for the girl with the unforgettable voice. When he found Ariel, he hoped she was the one. But she could not speak, let alone sing, so he decided she wasn't.

Still, this beautiful girl needed help. Eric invited her to be his guest.

At the castle, Ariel was given fine clothes to wear, and treated like an honoured guest.

And soon, just as she had hoped, the Prince seemed to be falling in love with her.

On Ariel's second evening as a human, Eric took her for a romantic boat ride in the moonlight. He was just about to kiss her, when Flotsam and Jetsam overturned the boat, and ruined the mood.

"That was close!" Ursula exclaimed as she watched the scene in her crystal ball.

She decided it was time for drastic action. So she disguised herself as a beautiful girl named Vanessa, and wore Ariel's voice in a locket around her neck. Then she made her appearance beneath the castle's walls, and let the voice work its magic.

When Eric heard her voice, he thought Vanessa must be the girl who had saved his life.

Eric made up his mind to marry Vanessa the very next day. The wedding would take place at sea, on his ship.

Vanessa was alone in her cabin before the ceremony, preening in the mirror, when Scuttle happened to look through the porthole. To Scuttle's surprise, he saw Vanessa's reflection in the mirror and realised she was really the Sea Witch!

"Soon I'll have that little mermaid and her handsome prince, and the ocean will be mine!" he heard Ursula gloat.

"I've got to tell Ariel!" Scuttle decided.

Scuttle found Ariel and Sebastian on the shore, and passed on the horrible news. Then, while Ariel hurried to the ship, Scuttle organised a flock of birds and sea creatures.

Scuttle's army attacked Vanessa the moment she stepped onto the deck for the wedding ceremony. The locket broke from her neck, and Ariel's voice was released to its rightful owner, just as Ariel climbed aboard the ship.

"Oh, Eric..." Ariel said, finally able to speak again.

"It was you all the time!" Eric exclaimed.

But it was too late. "You belong to me now," the Sea Witch screamed at Ariel, as she resumed her monstrous form.

The sun dipped swiftly below the horizon. The Little Mermaid's three days were up. The wedding guests stared in shock as Ariel became a mermaid again. In a moment, she and Ursula vanished beneath the waves.

Back under the sea, Ursula showed Triton his imprisoned daughter and the signed contract.

"However, I'll give Ariel her freedom — in exchange for yours," she offered.

King Triton loved his little daughter so much that he agreed to the bargain.

"At last!" Ursula crowed. "I am sole ruler of all the ocean!" Then she used Triton's own magic trident to transform him into a pathetic sea creature, stuck forever in her captivity.

Meanwhile, Prince Eric had gone in search of Ariel. "I lost her once. I'm not going to lose her again," he vowed.

Now, his harpoon flashed through the water, directed straight at the Sea Witch.

As soon as Ursula caught sight of the prince, she aimed the trident. But Ariel managed to throw Ursula off balance, so the deadly rays hit the Sea Witch's own evil eels instead of Eric.

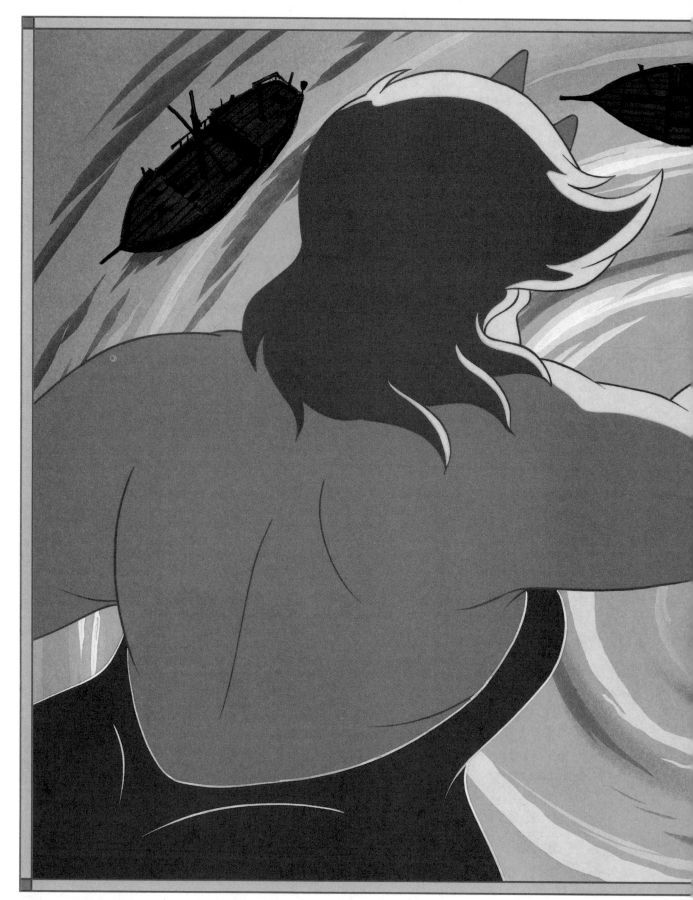

Ursula was so enraged that her evil heart grew. And so did she, until she towered over the ocean.

"You pitiful fools!" she shrieked. "Now you will feel the power of the Sea Witch!"

Lightning flashed. Great waves swept over the sea, tossing up ancient shipwrecks from the seabed.

Eric managed to climb onto one of the
wrecks. He steered it towards the
mountainous form of the Sea Witch and
impaled her on the ship's sharp bowsprit.
With a bloodcurdling scream, Ursula
disintegrated into a patch of bubbling
black ooze.

With Ursula's destruction, Triton regained his power as king of the sea. At once, he went searching for his beloved daughter.

He found her on her favourite rock, staring longingly at Eric, who had been washed safely onto the beach.

And so King Triton granted Ariel her dearest wish. He made her human forever, so that she could marry Prince Eric.

The wedding was held aboard Eric's ship, with all the merpeople looking on from the sea.

Though King Triton was sad to know his Little Mermaid would no longer live with him under the sea, his heart was lightened knowing that she would be forever happy with the man of her dreams.

The edition containing the full text of *Bambi, A Life in the Woods*
by Felix Salten, is published by Simon & Schuster.

213

There was great excitement in the forest. The sound of happy voices awakened Friend Owl. He flew towards the voices, and saw a newborn fawn huddled against his mother.

Since early morning, Thumper the rabbit had been spreading the good news. "Wake up! The little prince is born!" he had announced. The forest animals had come from near and far to admire the new fawn.

"Well, this is quite an occasion!" Friend Owl said to the new mother. "You're to be congratulated!"

"What are you going to call him?" Thumper asked.

"Well," the fawn's mother replied, "I think I'll call him Bambi."

As soon as little Bambi realised how his legs
worked, he set out to explore the clearing
in the company of his new friends.

Thumper was proud to teach him what he knew.
"Those are birds," he explained.

"Burr," Bambi said, trying to imitate Thumper.

Then something else caught the fawn's eye.
"Bird!" he said proudly.

"No, that's a butterfly," Thumper explained.

"But-but-butterfly!" Bambi repeated.

Bambi was very happy in the forest. He made friends, and his mother taught him all sorts of things: which plants could be eaten, and where water would always be found.

The little fawn listened carefully, and asked all sorts of questions. But then he was ready to play.

One day, he saw a wide open space, and ran towards it.

"Bambi! Wait!" his mother cried, calling him back. "You must never rush out on the meadow. There might be danger. There are no trees and bushes to hide us, so we have to be very careful."

She made Bambi wait in the forest, until she could make sure the meadow was safe.

Later, with his mother, Bambi found something interesting – a pool of still water. He leaned over, then backed away in confusion. Another fawn was looking right back at him from the water!

Bambi looked again and soon understood it was only his reflection. But then he saw a second reflection. What was going on? He ran to hide behind his mother.

"That's little Faline," his mother explained, as the other fawn approached.

"He's rather bashful, isn't he?" Faline remarked.

"Go ahead, Bambi. Say hello," his mother said, giving him a nudge.

It took a little encouragement, but soon Bambi was frolicking happily with his new friend Faline.

Bambi met some other deer, too, for the meadow was a popular place with all the forest animals. He even saw some deer with beautiful antlers on their heads. They were young stags, he learned, and one day he would have antlers like theirs.

Suddenly, the fawns' play was interrupted by the sound of thundering hooves.

A majestic stag appeared, and all the deer fell silent. It was the Great Prince of the Forest. He looked straight at Bambi for a moment, then walked away.

But a few moments later, the Great Prince ran back through the meadow. He had sensed danger, and returned to warn the other deer.

Bambi heard his mother calling him to run, but he didn't know which way to go.

Then the Great Prince of the Forest appeared beside him, and led Bambi to safety. Just as they slipped into the woods, they heard the sound of gunshots behind them.

Bambi hid in thick brush, in the deepest part of the forest, until he heard his mother calling.

"Come on out," she said. "It's safe now. We don't have to hide any longer."

"What happened, Mother? Why did we all run?" Bambi asked.

"Man was in the forest," she explained.

One morning a few days later, the cold awakened Bambi. When he looked out, he saw a thick white blanket covering the ground.

 "Mother, look!" he cried. "What's all that white stuff?"

"It's snow," she explained. "Winter has come."

Bambi set off to explore this new world of white.

"Hello, Bambi!" Thumper called. "Look what I can do!" Thumper took off at speed, then went sliding across the surface of a frozen pond.

"Come on, it's all right — look! The water's stiff!" he told Bambi.

"Yippee!" Bambi shouted, but as soon as he hit the ice, his legs went flying out from under him.

Thumper helped him get up. "You've got to watch both ends at the same time," he explained, and showed him how it was done.

Snow continued to fall. It covered everything, and soon it became difficult to find plants to eat. His mother taught him how to gnaw the bark off trees and dig up roots.

"I'm awfully hungry, Mother," Bambi said.

"Yes, I know," his mother said. She explained that winter would not last forever.

One day, the deer discovered some new spring grass peeking up through the snow in the meadow. They were munching happily, when suddenly, Bambi's mother stopped. She had sensed danger.

"Bambi!" she said urgently. "Quick! The thicket!"

Bambi dashed toward the thicket with his mother close behind.

"Run, Bambi! Run and hide! Don't look back!" his mother cried.

Bambi ran deep into the forest. Terrified and out of breath, he finally stopped, looked back and called his mother. But she wasn't there behind him. He was alone! Bambi began to cry.

"Mother, where are you?" Bambi called.

Suddenly the Great Prince of the Forest appeared beside him. "Your mother can't be with you anymore. Man has taken her away. Now you must be brave," he said. "Come, my son."

So little Bambi followed his father into the snow.

The days passed, and Bambi began to forget his sadness. By the time spring came again, he had grown into a magnificent young stag.

One morning, Bambi was out roaming with Thumper and Flower the skunk, when they noticed some birds acting strangely.

"They're twitterpated," Friend Owl explained. "Nearly everybody gets twitterpated in the springtime. It could even happen to you!"

"Not me!" the three friends vowed.

But soon Flower met a pretty little girl skunk, and began acting foolishly.

Then Thumper met a cute female rabbit, and got twitterpated too.

Bambi walked on alone, shaking his head in amazement. What was the matter with his two friends? Then he heard a voice say, "Hello, Bambi. Don't you remember me?"

It was Faline. But she had changed somehow. And for some reason, Bambi felt too bashful to speak.

Then Faline nuzzled him. And that was it. He was twitterpated too.

Bambi was following Faline through the woods, when suddenly they ran into a fierce young stag named Ronno.

Ronno had long ago decided that Faline would be his mate. Faline was frightened for Bambi, but Bambi realised that if he wanted to be with Faline, he would have to fight.

The two young stags hurled themselves at each other. The forest was filled with the sound of their antlers clashing. Finally, however, Bambi drove Ronno away.

Bambi and Faline looked tenderly at each other, knowing that nothing could separate them now.

Days passed, and autumn came. The animals of the forest were nervous. Man was in the forest again.

All the animals tried to stay hidden in the thickest parts of the forest. But some of the men had brought dogs. One day, the dogs chased Faline, nearly catching her. Bambi barely managed to fight off the dogs and rescue her, but he was seriously injured.

Too weak to move, Bambi lay where he had fallen. Suddenly he noticed a strange odour in the air. Fire!

"Get up, Bambi," he heard the Great Prince of the Forest say. Bambi struggled to his feet. "Now, follow me."

The fire spread rapidly, burning more and more of the forest. The animals raced to escape the flames and reach safety. It was hard to breathe because of the smoke.

But at last Bambi and the Great Prince of the Forest reached the river, and waded across.

On the opposite bank other animals waited, watching the approaching fire. Faline was among the lucky animals who had escaped. "Bambi!" she cried.

After the great forest fire, the forest slowly healed.

And the following spring, Faline brought not only one, but two lovely fawns into the world.

News once again travelled quickly through the forest: Bambi was a father! All the animals gathered to admire the newborn fawns.

"Prince Bambi ought to be very proud," Friend Owl remarked when he saw the newborns.

Far above Friend Owl, the Great Prince Bambi looked down at his new family. He was proud, indeed.

# POCAHONTAS

"**W**here is Pocahontas?" asked Chief Powhatan. Everyone in the village had turned out to welcome home their leader and his brave warriors — everyone, that is, except Powhatan's beloved daughter, Pocahontas.

As usual, Pocahontas was off on an adventure with her two friends, Meeko the raccoon, and a hummingbird called Flit.

Her best friend, Nakoma, eventually found Pocahontas standing on her favourite cliff, lost in thought. "Your father's back!" Nakoma called.

Pocahontas excitedly headed home. She was anxious to tell her father about the dream she kept having, a dream about a spinning arrow. She knew it meant something exciting was going to happen. But what?

Powhatan smiled when he heard his daughter's account of her dream and its meaning. "Something exciting *is* about to happen," he said. "Kocoum has asked to seek your hand in marriage." Then he gave his daughter a necklace. It was the same necklace her mother had worn at *her* wedding to Powhatan many years before.

Although Pocahontas was greatly moved by her father's gift, she did not want to marry Kocoum. He was certainly the bravest and most handsome of the young warriors. But he never smiled. And besides, she had a feeling her dream was pointing her down another path.

So she went to see Grandmother Willow for advice. "What is my path?" Pocahontas asked. "How am I ever going to find it?"

"All around you are spirits, child," the wise tree spirit said. "They live in the earth, the water, the sky. If you listen, they will guide you."

As if in response to Grandmother Willow's words, a breeze began to blow. Pocahontas ran to the shore and climbed a cliff, hoping to hear what the wind was telling her.

That's when she saw a sight she had never seen before. It was the *Susan Constant*, its sails flapping in the breeze. The ship had sailed all the way from England, bringing settlers to the land where Pocahontas lived.

The first one off the ship was John Smith. Smith was anxious to explore this new land, especially after being cooped up on the ship for several months.

He had been given a special assignment by Governor Ratcliffe, the leader of the expedition. "I'm counting on you to make sure that any Indians we find won't get in our way," Ratcliffe had said.

"If they're anything like the ones I've seen before, it's nothing I can't handle," Smith had replied.

Now, on shore, Smith wandered quite close to the spot where Pocahontas had hidden herself. Meeko the raccoon couldn't resist the chance to investigate the stranger, and ran out to greet him.

"You're a strange looking fellow," Smith said, holding out a biscuit.

Meeko was so excited with the gift, that he nearly gave away Pocahontas's hiding place. But just then, a bugle sounded, calling Smith back to the other settlers.

Smith had been summoned to watch Governor Ratcliffe plant the British flag. Ratcliffe said he was claiming the new land for his king and country. But all he really cared about was the gold and other riches he hoped to find.

Ratcliffe was ruthless and ambitious. He had promised the settlers freedom and prosperity in a new land. But he was willing to risk their lives for his own personal gain.

The only living thing Ratcliffe seemed to care about was his pug dog, Percy. Percy was so spoiled that he was carried around on a velvet cushion, and fed better food than the settlers were given. Little Meeko soon made it his ambition to share Percy's luxuries.

After the flag-planting ceremony, Ratcliffe had the settlers begin to dig for gold.

Meanwhile, a party of warriors had spotted the settlers putting up their encampment near the shore. When they reported this to their chief, Powhatan asked Kekata, the village medicine man, to find out what the arrival of the white men might mean.

Kekata threw some powder on the fire. The smoke that rose from the flames took the shape of hungry wolves and of soldiers with weapons that spouted fire.

Powhatan realised the situation called for caution.

"Take some men to the river to observe these visitors," he ordered Kocoum. "Let us hope they do not intend to stay."

Meanwhile, John Smith was exploring the forest, when he sensed that he was not alone. Turning, he saw Pocahontas through the mist of a waterfall. They stared at each other for a long moment, before Pocahontas darted away.

"No, wait, please..." Smith called after her.

Then Pocahontas remembered what Grandmother Willow had said — to listen with her heart to the voices around her. So she decided to stop and listen to this stranger.

As they got to know each other, Pocahontas realised that Smith had some odd ideas. For instance, he thought the Indians were savages. And he did not understand that all the parts of nature — people, animals, plants, even the wind and clouds — were alive, and connected to each other.

So she showed John Smith her world. Slowly, he started to see the colours and shapes of the wind, and the rest of nature, just as she did. When they parted at the end of the day, neither one wanted to say good-bye.

Soon the tension between the settlers and Indians began to worsen. Ratcliffe had found no gold, and was furious. He was sure the Indians were hiding it all.

There had already been one confrontation near the settlers' encampment. One of the Indian warriors who had gone to observe the settlers with Kocoum had been shot and wounded.

"These white men are dangerous!" Powhatan said, and gave orders that no one was to go near the settlers again.

But Pocahontas ignored his order. She even ignored the warning of her best friend Nakoma, who told her to stay away from John Smith. Instead, when Smith came to meet her while she was out picking corn, she quickly left with him, leading him to Grandmother Willow's glade.

That's when she found out that the settlers had come for gold. "What is gold?" Pocahontas asked.

Once Smith had explained, Pocahontas told him that the only gold the Indians had was the golden corn they grew in their fields.

They were still talking when Grandmother Willow joined the conversation. "Hello, John Smith," she said.

Smith was shaken. "Pocahontas, that tree is talking to me," he blurted out.

"Don't be frightened," the tree spirit told him. "My bark is worse than my bite."

Soon, Grandmother Willow and John Smith were chatting away as if they had known each other for years. Pocahontas was pleased that Grandmother Willow approved of her new friend.

Suddenly, they were interrupted by the shouts of two settlers who were looking for Smith. Smith realised he had to get back to the settlement.

When Pocahontas reached home, she discovered that the Indians were preparing for battle. She went to her father and begged him to talk to the settlers, instead of fighting.

"It's not that simple," Powhatan replied. He was convinced that the settlers were not interested in talking.

When Smith returned to the settlement, he tried to explain to Governor Ratcliffe and the others that the Indians had no gold, only corn. He also explained that the corn was food, and that the Indians would be happy to share it.

But the Governor wasn't interested in even looking at the corn Smith had brought him.

Ratcliffe made his position absolutely clear. "Anyone who so much as looks at an Indian without killing him on sight will be tried for treason and hanged," he said.

Smith still believed that it might be possible to keep the peace with the Indians. So that night, he met secretly with Pocahontas at the enchanted glade.

Pocahontas suggested that Smith should come to her village, and talk to her father. He was reluctant, until Grandmother Willow convinced him that someone had to take the first step towards peace.

"All right. Let's go talk to your father," Smith said. Pocahontas was overjoyed, and threw her arms around him.

Just then, however, Kocoum stepped into the glade. Nakoma had sent Kocoum after Pocahontas, because she was worried for her friend's safety. When the young warrior saw Pocahontas in the arms of Smith, he attacked.

Smith's friend Thomas arrived just in time to see Kocoum with a knife raised against Smith. He fired his musket, and Kocoum fell to the ground, dead.

"Thomas, get out of here!" Smith yelled.

When a party of warriors appeared moments later, they dragged Smith away.

Powhatan condemned Smith to die at sunrise. And he had harsh words for Pocahontas. "Because of your foolishness, Kocoum is dead. You have shamed your father!" he said.

Meanwhile, Thomas carried the news of Smith's capture back to the settlement.

Ratcliffe used the information to inspire the settlers to fight. This was what happened, he told them, when someone tried to befriend the Indians. He soon had them fired up and ready for battle.

Meanwhile, Pocahontas had wandered back to the enchanted glade. She was heartbroken, but could not think of any way to help Smith.

She was holding Smith's compass, which he had given to little Meeko. The compass arrow began spinning wildly, then suddenly stopped. It was pointing towards the sunrise... and John Smith.

Pocahontas realised it was the arrow from her dream. She began to run in the direction the arrow was pointing.

Just before sunrise, the Indians arrived at the place of execution. The settlers were also marching, armed and angry, to the same spot. It seemed that nothing could prevent bloodshed now.

Then, just as Powhatan raised a huge club over Smith, Pocahontas appeared.

She threw herself over Smith and shouted, "No! If you kill him, you'll have to kill me too! Look around you. This is where the path of hatred has brought us."

No one moved. Then Pocahontas said, "You have the power to change that, Father."

Powhatan heard the wisdom of his daughter's words. "From this day forward there will be no more killing," he announced. "Let us be guided instead to a place of peace."

When the Indian warriors put down their weapons, Ratcliffe yelled, "Now's our chance, men. Fire!"

But the settlers had finally understood how greedy Ratcliffe was. They lowered their weapons too.

In desperation, Ratcliffe reached for a gun and fired at Powhatan. John Smith hurled himself in front of the chief, and was shot instead.

The settlers were enraged. They grabbed Ratcliffe, put him in chains, and dragged him to the ship.

The next day, the settlers prepared the *Susan Constant* to set sail for England. The Indians brought blankets and food for their journey.

John Smith lay on a stretcher, ready to be carried on board. Thomas told Pocahontas that Smith would die if he stayed behind. "Going back is his only chance," Thomas explained.

Powhatan placed his own cloak over Smith. "You are always welcome among our people," he said. "Thank you, my brother."

Then Pocahontas approached Smith. She had brought a small pouch for him. "It's from Grandmother Willow's bark," she said. "It will help with the pain."

"Come with me," John Smith begged.

Pocahontas looked to her father for advice. "You must choose your own path," Powhatan said.

Then Pocahontas looked at the Indians sharing food with the settlers. It was the first sign of peace, and she had made it happen.

Suddenly, Pocahontas realised what her dream had meant, and what her path must be. She would continue working for peace between her people and the newcomers.

As Pocahontas watched the *Susan Constant* sail away, a gentle wind whispered in her ear. She knew that the same wind would carry John Smith safely home.

It was Christmas at Jim Dear and Darling's house. There were so many presents under the tree that Darling didn't know where to start.

Jim Dear handed his wife a hat box that was big enough to hold a large hat. From the way the bottom of the box sagged, it looked as if the hat were quite heavy.

Darling unwrapped the box. Inside, was a beautiful cocker spaniel puppy, wearing a large red bow.

"Do you like her, Darling?" asked Jim Dear.

"Oh, I love her," Darling answered. "What a perfectly beautiful little lady."

So "Lady" became her name.

Lady grew up loved and pampered. She had a few simple jobs around the house, such as bringing in the newspaper and making sure the blackbirds did not sit too long on the front lawn.

She had plenty of time to spend with her neighbours, Jock the Scottie and Trusty the bloodhound.

One day, Lady told her two friends that Jim Dear and Darling had been treating her differently lately. For instance, they didn't want to play with her any more. They were not taking her on her regular walks. And mysteriously, Darling had begun knitting tiny little clothes.

Jock and Trusty knew right away what was causing the odd behaviour. "Darling is expecting a baby," they said.

"A baby?" Lady asked, bewildered. Her two friends were trying to explain, when a scruffy-looking dog named Tramp joined in.

Tramp just happened to be passing through the neighbourhood. When he overheard Lady mention a baby, he felt obliged to warn her. "Better watch out!" he said. "When the baby moves in, the dog moves out!"

Sure enough, a few months later a baby was born to Jim Dear and Darling. Lady was happy for them.

But before long, things changed for the worse. It began when Jim Dear and Darling decided to go away for a holiday. They arranged for someone named Aunt Sarah to look after the baby.

Aunt Sarah would not let Lady anywhere near the baby. And she brought along two Siamese cats, Si and Am, who immediately started making trouble. First they tried to get their paws on the fish. Then they went after the canary!

Lady was trying to stop them when Aunt Sarah heard the commotion they were making. "What's going on down there?" she called, hurrying to the living room.

By the time she arrived, Si and Am were sitting quietly, as if they were completely innocent. Aunt Sarah jumped to the conclusion that Lady was responsible for the mess.

"Wicked animal! Attacking my poor innocent little angels!" she scolded and hauled Lady off to the pet shop.

"I want a muzzle, a good strong muzzle," Aunt Sarah told the pet shop owner.

Lady had never worn a muzzle, and she was frightened when the man put it over her face. She struggled wildly and finally managed to wriggle out of Aunt Sarah's arms.

Then she made a dash for the street. She didn't care where she went. She just wanted to get away from Aunt Sarah.

Lady ran blindly across a street filled with traffic, then turned up an alley. That's when a gang of stray dogs saw her and chased after her, barking and snarling.

Lady ran as fast as she could, but the strays chased her into a dead-end street. She was cornered.

Fortunately, Tramp had stopped for a snack near the alley. He saw Lady race by and hurried to defend her.

While Lady cowered behind a barrel, Tramp lunged at one of the attacking dogs, then another.

The vicious strays fought furiously, but finally they realised they were no match for Tramp and fled back down the alley.

Tramp remembered Lady from his short visit in her front yard. "What are you doing on this side of the tracks?" he asked.

Lady could only look at him sadly; the muzzle prevented her from talking.

"You poor kid! We've got to get this off," Tramp said. "I know just the place."

Tramp led Lady to the city zoo. At first, he thought they might get an alligator to chew through the muzzle, but his jaws looked too dangerous.

Then they spied a beaver cutting logs. The beaver was reluctant to interrupt his work until Tramp convinced him that the muzzle would make a handy log puller.

So the beaver gnawed through the strap, and finally, Lady was free.

The beaver examined the muzzle carefully. "I'll have to make certain
it's satisfactory before we settle on a price," he said.

"It's all yours, friend. You can keep it," Tramp said and rushed away leaving the beaver content with his new tool.

With the muzzle off, Lady was able to tell Tramp the whole story about Aunt Sarah, her cats, and the muzzle.

"That's what comes of tying yourself down to one family," Tramp said. "I'll show you what I mean."

It was Wednesday, the day Tramp always ate at Tony's Restaurant. Tony was glad to see him and had some juicy bones all ready for him. But when he saw that Tramp had brought along a lady friend, he invited the two dogs to stay for a romantic dinner.

Soon Lady and Tramp were eating spaghetti, while Tony and the waiter played love songs for them. By the time they had finished dinner, Lady and Tramp had begun to fall in love.

That night, Tramp and Lady fell asleep in the moonlight. The next morning, Tramp asked Lady to stay with him. He described a life of freedom and excitement, and Lady felt very tempted. But in the end, she decided she really ought to go home. So Tramp offered to accompany her.

On the way, they passed a flock of chickens, and Tramp saw a chance to show Lady just how exciting life could be. "Ever chase chickens?" he said. "Come on. We'll just stir them up a bit."

The angry chickens made such a noise that their owner soon came running. Tramp was familiar with the routine and easily escaped. But when he turned to see if Lady was behind him, he realised she had been caught and taken to the dog pound.

Poor Lady! The scruffy dogs in the pound teased her about her fancy collar until she was ready to cry.

As it turned out, the collar was Lady's salvation. One of the dog catchers noticed that she had a licence and phoned her home.

So Lady was taken back to her own house, but this time, she was not even allowed inside. Instead, Aunt Sarah tied her in the yard on a short chain.

Jock and Trusty came to cheer her up, but she was so ashamed she could barely speak.

Then Tramp arrived, bringing a bone as a gift. "It wasn't my fault..." he tried to explain.

But Lady was furious with him for getting her into trouble. She told him she did not want anything more to do with him. "And take this with you," she said, tossing the bone after him.

That night, Lady was lying forlornly next to her doghouse when she heard scrabbling sounds from the woodpile. A big rat crawled out, heading for the house.

Lady charged after him, growling, but her chain stopped her short. The rat scrambled up a trellis. Then it scuttled toward the baby's window!

Lady barked furiously, yanking at her chain.

"Stop that racket!" Aunt Sarah shouted, but Lady kept barking.

Tramp had lingered nearby and came running. "What's wrong?" he asked.

"A rat!" Lady panted. "Upstairs. In the baby's room!"

Tramp raced through the dog door and up the stairs. Lady broke free of her chain and followed. They reached the baby's room just in time to see the rat inches from the baby. Tramp pounced.

In the excitement that followed, Tramp and the rat knocked over furniture, pulled down curtains, and toppled the cot!

By the time Aunt Sarah arrived, the rat was nowhere to be seen. Lady and Tramp were standing guard proudly over the baby, who was gurgling happily.

"You vicious brutes!" Aunt Sarah shrieked. She thought Lady and Tramp were trying to hurt the baby, so she pushed Tramp into a closet with a broom and slammed the door. Then she chased Lady into the basement and went to call the dog pound.

Jim Dear and Darling arrived home as the dogcatcher was loading Tramp into the pound wagon. "If you want my advice, you'll destroy that animal at once!" they heard Aunt Sarah say.

"Don't worry, Ma'am," the dogcatcher replied. "We've been after this one for months."

"What's going on here?" Jim Dear asked, confused.

"Just picking up a stray," the dogcatcher said. "Caught him attacking a baby."

"Good heavens!" Jim cried. He and Darling raced to check on the baby. When they reached the baby's room, Lady showed them the dead rat, and they realised what had really happened.

Meanwhile, Trusty and Jock were trying to find Tramp. Trusty sniffed out the trail of the pound wagon. "We'll track them down," he said.

It was raining, and Trusty had some difficulty trailing the scent through the puddles. But finally the dogs caught up, then dashed in front of the horses pulling the pound wagon.

"Get out of here!" the dogcatcher yelled at them. "Go on, you! Get away!"

But the two dogs persisted, until finally the excited horses reared up, and the wagon tipped over.

Meanwhile, back at the house, Jim Dear and Lady had jumped into a taxi and raced to the pound to save Tramp.

When the pound wagon rolled back to its upright position, Tramp looked through the bars. Lady jumped out of the taxi and ran towards him.

That was the last night Tramp would ever have to worry about the dogcatcher because the next morning Jim Dear and Darling bought him a collar and a licence of his own. He and Lady settled down, and Tramp quickly discovered that having only one home had its advantages.

When Christmas came again at Jim Dear and Darling's house, there were four mischievous puppies under the tree. Of course, the loyal friends Jock and Trusty joined the celebration, too.

And can you guess who sent dog biscuits as a Christmas present? Nasty old Aunt Sarah.

Peter Pan chose to visit the Darling house because there were people there who believed in him.

Mrs. Darling believed Peter Pan was the spirit of youth. The boys, John and Michael, believed Peter Pan was a real person. They made him the hero of all their games. As for Wendy, their older sister, she was the supreme authority on Peter Pan. She knew everything about him. Even Nana, the nursemaid, believed in Peter, although being a dog, she kept her opinion of him to herself.

Mr. Darling was the only one who didn't believe. "Absolute poppycock!" he blurted when anyone mentioned Peter Pan. For Mr. Darling, the last straw came when he discovered the boys had drawn a pirate map on his last clean shirt front and hidden his cuff links.

The boys explained that they had been playing Peter Pan and Captain Hook, and the cuff links were buried treasure. But Mr. Darling didn't want to hear a word about it. As far as he was concerned, it was all Wendy's fault. "Stuffing the boys with a lot of silly stories!" he said.

So he decreed that it was time Wendy had a room of her own. "I mean it, young lady. This is your last night in the nursery!" he ordered to everyone's dismay. And since he was still in a temper, he fired the dog from her job as nursemaid, too, and tied her outside.

Wendy was troubled by her father's outburst, especially the part when he had told her she was going to have to grow up.

"But I don't want to grow up," she told her mother.

"Don't worry about it anymore tonight," her mother said.

John and Michael were upset too about Nana, Peter Pan, and losing Wendy from the nursery.

"Don't judge your father too harshly," Mrs. Darling told the children as she kissed them goodnight. "He really loves you very much."

Moments after Mr. and Mrs. Darling left for the theatre, Peter Pan hopped through the nursery window. Right behind him was Tinker Bell, although you wouldn't have known it unless you'd looked very closely because at the moment, she appeared only as a golden glow.

They had come for Peter Pan's shadow. Peter had become separated from it on his last visit to the Darling house, and Nana had taken it.

"Must be here somewhere," Peter said, looking around the nursery. After some searching, he found it in the drawer where Wendy had put it after she'd found Nana chewing on it.

The shadow didn't want to be caught. It flew out of the drawer and made Peter chase it around the room, thumping into things. The noise woke up Wendy. "I knew you'd come back!" she cried to Peter.

Wendy knew just what to do with the reluctant shadow — she'd sew it back on! So she got out her sewing kit.

Meanwhile, Peter explained how Nana had grabbed his shadow while he was lurking on the window ledge, listening to Wendy's stories.

"My stories? But they're all about you!" Wendy cried.

"Of course. That's why I like them," Peter said.

Wendy wasn't too happy to tell Peter the news that there would be no more stories. "I have to grow up tomorrow. Tonight's my last night in the nursery," she explained.

"I won't have it," Peter cried. "Come on. We're going to Never Land. You'll never grow up there!"

It took only a minute to wake John and Michael...

...and another few minutes for the Darling children to learn how to fly. It was quite easy to do, really, as long as you had a bit of Tinker Bell's pixie dust. Then they were on their way to Never Land.

The island of Never Land is an extremely long distance from the city of London, or any other city for that matter. But because of the pixie dust, it was no time at all before the Darling children spotted it in the sea below.

"Oh Peter! It's just as I've always dreamed it would be!" Wendy cried.

From Wendy's stories, the children already knew that Never Land was home to Peter and his Lost Boys, as well as an Indian tribe and a number of mermaids. They also knew that Peter's mortal enemy, Captain Hook, kept his pirate ship anchored in the harbour. And there it was, down below.

None of the Darling children was prepared for the welcome they received from the pirates. "Look out!" Peter cried as a cannonball came hurtling towards them from the ship's deck. Luckily the Darling children had already flown quickly out of the way.

"Quick, Tink! Take Wendy and the boys to the island," Peter shouted. "I'll stay here and draw Hook's fire."

Captain Hook and Peter had been enemies for a long time. As far as the pirate was concerned, Peter was the cause of all his misfortunes. He even blamed Peter for the fact that a crocodile followed him continually. The Crocodile had swallowed Hook's left hand a few years earlier and had been waiting for another taste of him ever since.

Fortunately, the Crocodile had also swallowed an alarm clock. The tick-tock of the clock warned Hook whenever the Crocodile was around. Still, Hook was terrified each time he saw it. He relied on the pirate Smee to keep the Crocodile as far from him as possible.

Hook had vowed to find Peter Pan's hide-out, so that he could get revenge. He had sent his pirates to search Mermaid Lagoon, Cannibal Cove, and everywhere else he had been able to think of.

By now the pirates were fed up. They wanted to get back to buccaneering. But Hook couldn't stop poring over the map desperately searching for Peter Pan.

"I've got it!" he finally cried, pointing at the Indian encampment. "Tiger Lily! The Chief's daughter. She'll know where Pan is hiding!"

But before Hook could arrange to kidnap Tiger Lily, Peter and the Darling children flew into view, and Hook had ordered his pirates to fire the cannons at them.

Tinker Bell flew down towards Never Land, dodging cannon balls. Wendy and the boys followed far behind. "Wait! We can't keep up!" Wendy cried. But Tinker Bell thought Peter was paying far too much attention to Wendy. So she flew ahead and told the Lost Boys to shoot Wendy down.

Fortunately, Wendy was not hurt. But Peter was furious when he found out what had happened. "You blockheads," he said. "I bring you a mother to tell you stories, and you shoot her down."

Since Tinker Bell was to blame, he charged her with high treason and banished her for a week.

Later, John and Michael said they would like to see some Indians. "All right," Peter agreed. "John, you be the leader." So John led an expedition of Lost Boys through the jungle. Almost at once, they found some Indians. And the next thing they knew, they were tied to a totem pole.

John and Michael were worried, but the Lost Boys weren't. It was a game, they explained. "When we win, we turn them loose. When they win, they turn us loose."

But this time, the Chief wouldn't let them go. He thought the Lost Boys were the ones who had kidnapped Tiger Lily. And if she wasn't back by sunset, the boys would be burned at the stake.

Meanwhile, Peter had taken Wendy to meet some mermaids. But the mermaids ignored Wendy completely. Instead, they flirted with Peter and begged him to tell them one of his adventures. Peter started to recount the time he had been surrounded by fifty pirates when Wendy lost patience. "Oh, Peter!" she interrupted.

"Who's she?" one of the mermaids asked. "What's she doing here?" said another. "And in her nightdress, too!" a third remarked rudely, splashing water on Wendy's nightie.

Other mermaids tried to pull Wendy into the water. She was just about to smack one of them with a seashell when Peter stopped her. "They're just having a little fun. Weren't you, girls?" he said.

"That's all. We were only trying to drown her," one of the mermaids said.

"Well if you think for one minute..." Wendy started to say, but Peter put his hand over her mouth. He had just noticed Captain Hook and Smee rowing off in the distance towards Skull Rock,... and they had Tiger Lily with them!

Quickly, Peter and Wendy flew off to get a closer look.

Captain Hook had a proposal for Tiger Lily whom he had tied in a place where she would soon be covered by the rising tide. "You tell me the hiding place of Peter Pan, and I shall set you free," Hook said. Tiger Lily was silent. "You'd better talk, my dear," Hook urged, "for soon the tide will be in, and then it will be too late."

"Stay here, Wendy, and watch the fun," Peter said, leaving her high on a cliff, out of danger. He flew behind a rock and lured Hook away from Tiger Lily by imitating the voice of a water spirit. "Beware, Captain Hook. Beware!" Peter intoned.

But Hook was not fooled for long. "Come down, boy, if you've a taste for cold steel!" he shouted. In response, Peter flew down to the Captain and did a little dance on the end of Hook's sword.

This was too much for Hook. He sprang into action. In the sword fight that followed, Peter managed to back Hook off the edge of a cliff.

The Crocodile was waiting below, its jaws gaping. Hook almost ran on top of the water in his effort to reach Smee and the boat!

Peter and Wendy rescued Tiger Lily and took her back to the Indian camp.

The chief released the Lost Boys and declared in sign language that Peter Pan was a mighty warrior for rescuing Tiger Lily. As a reward, he gave Peter an Indian headdress and a new title: Little Flying Eagle. Afterwards, John was permitted to ask hundreds of questions about Indian lore.

Meanwhile, Smee had managed to pry Hook loose from the jaws of the Crocodile and rowed him back to the ship with the Crocodile snapping behind them all the way.

The terrible ordeal had exhausted Hook. He was seriously considering giving up on getting his revenge on Peter Pan. He would go back to his normal life, scuttling ships and cutting throats.

But then Smee told him about the rumour that was going around: Tinker Bell was jealous of Wendy. She had tried to kill Wendy, and Peter Pan had ended up banishing the little pixie!

"That's it, Smee! That's it!" Hook shouted. Quickly he dispatched Smee to find Tinker Bell.

Smee found her sitting dejectedly on a branch. He scooped her into his cap. "Begging your pardon, Miss Bell," he said, "but Captain Hook would like a word with you."

Hook was devious. He told Tinker Bell that he admitted defeat, and was leaving the island for good. He wanted Peter to know that he bore him no ill will, although he did think bringing Wendy to the island had been a mistake. "Rumour has it that already she has come between you and Peter," Hook said slyly.

Tinker Bell burst into tears, and Hook pretended to be sympathetic. Then, as if he had just thought of the idea, he offered a solution to her problem. "We'll get rid of Wendy!" he said. Now, if only he knew where Peter lived...

Tinker Bell agreed to show Hook the location on the map if he promised not to lay a finger or a hook on Peter Pan. Captain Hook gave her his word, and Tinker Bell traced the path to Peter's hide-out on the map.

Hook thanked Tinker Bell, then trapped her inside a lantern!

Meanwhile, Wendy and the boys had returned to Peter's hide-out. "Michael, take off that war paint and get ready for bed," Wendy said. "We're going home in the morning."

"Oh, Wendy, we don't want to go home," Michael whined.

"Let's stop pretending and be practical," Wendy said. "You need a mother. We all do."

But the boys seemed to have forgotten what a mother was. Wendy had to remind them. "A mother is the most wonderful person in the world..." she began.

By the time she had finished, John and Michael longed to go home. Even the Lost Boys, who had not seen their mothers in a very long time, felt sad and wanted to go home, too. So they all decided to leave Never Land that very night.

Peter was the only one who wanted to stay in Never Land. "Go back, and grow up!" he told the others. "But I'm warning you — once you're grown up, you can never come back."

As the boys marched out the door, Wendy stayed behind for a moment. She wanted to say good-bye to Peter. But he just turned his back on her.

As soon as Wendy stepped out of the tree, she saw that her brothers and the Lost Boys had been captured by pirates. She had no time to react and was carried away.

"And now, Smee, to take care of Master Peter Pan," Hook said as he placed a gift-wrapped box in front of Peter's door. Then he rang the bell.

"Wouldn't it be more human-like to slit his throat?" Smee asked.

But Hook had given his word to Tinker Bell not to lay a finger on Peter Pan. Or a hook, for that matter. "And Captain Hook never breaks a promise," he said.

Back on the ship, Captain Hook gave the boys a simple choice: They could sign on as members of the pirate gang; or they could walk the plank.

The boys were all about to sign when Wendy stopped them. "Peter Pan will save us!" she said.

"I don't believe you are in on our little joke," Hook said. "A sort of a surprise package, you might say." The package he had left at Peter's door contained a bomb, Hook explained. And it was set to go off within the next few seconds.

Tinker Bell overheard the conversation. She struggled desperately and finally overturned the lantern, shattering the glass. Quickly, she flew off to warn Peter.

Peter had found the package and read the note on it. "To Peter, with love from Wendy. Do not open 'til six o'clock."

The clock on the wall of his underground home said twelve seconds to six, but Peter couldn't wait any longer. He was untying the ribbon when Tinker Bell flew in. "Hi Tink. Look what Wendy left!" Peter said.

The pixie tugged at the package, trying to get it away from him. "Hey, stop that! What's the matter with you?" Peter cried.

Tinker Bell jingled furiously. "Hook? A bomb? Don't be ridiculous!" Peter said. Then he noticed the smoke coming out of the package...

*Kaboom!* The force of the explosion rocked the ship in the harbour. Hook removed his hat and bowed his head for a moment. "So passeth a worthy opponent," he said. Then he turned to Wendy. "Which will it be, the pen or the plank?"

"We will never join your crew," Wendy replied.

"As you wish," said Hook. "Ladies first, my dear."

Wendy said, "Goodbye, boys," and she walked off the edge of the plank.

The pirates waited to hear the splash Wendy would make as she hit the water. It never came! A pirate looked over the side. "Not a ripple!" he said. "It's a jinx, that's what it is!"

It wasn't a jinx; it was Peter Pan. He had arrived just in time to save Wendy. They listened to the pirates' conversation from their perch on the anchor chain. Then Peter flew Wendy to the safety of the crow's nest and turned towards the pirates. He had business to conclude with Captain Hook.

Meanwhile, Captain Hook was yelling at the pirates. "You want a splash?" he asked his worried shipmates. "I'll give you a splash! Who's next?"

"You're next, Hook!" Peter said. "Say your prayers."

Hook was furious that Peter had escaped the bomb. He lunged at Peter with his sword, but Peter darted and dodged so quickly that the Captain got his hook stuck in the mast. While he struggled free, Peter had time to untie all the boys. They joined the battle.

"Down, you villain!" John yelled, whacking a pirate with his umbrella.

Peter Pan and Hook fought along the mast. Every time Hook got close, Peter would fly away. "You wouldn't dare fight old Hook man to man!" The Captain taunted. "You'd fly away like a cowardly sparrow!"

Peter hated being called a coward. He gave his word he would fight without flying. "No, Peter. It's a trick!" Wendy shouted.

Peter ignored Wendy's warning and fought on. Hook backed him to the end of a yardarm, and Peter nearly fell off. Wendy couldn't watch. She covered her eyes. Below, the Crocodile waited patiently.

Then Peter grabbed the skull and crossbones flag, and tangled Hook in it. Now the pirate was at his mercy. "Kill him!" the boys shouted.

Hook grovelled, "I'll go away forever! I'll do anything you say."

"All right," Peter said. "If you say you're a codfish."

"I'm a codfish," Hook said.

So Peter told Hook he was free to go. Then, as soon as Peter turned his back, Hook raised his arm to strike him with his hook. He missed, and lost his balance.

The Crocodile was ready for him.

"Hooray for Captain Pan!" the Lost Boys shouted.

Peter strutted across the deck like a Captain. "All right, you swabs," he said. "We're casting off! Heave those halyards." The boys scrambled back into the rigging.

"But, Peter," Wendy said. "Oh, that is, Captain Pan," she stuttered. "Could you tell me, sir, where we're sailing?"

"To London, madam," Peter replied.

"Michael! John! We're going home!" Wendy cried joyfully.

While the Lost Boys raised the anchor, Peter called to Tinker Bell. "Pixie dust," he ordered.

Tinker Bell saluted and sprinkled pixie dust over the deck and rails. The pirate ship began to glow. Then it rose slowly from the water until Never Land was far below.

When Mr. and Mrs. Darling got home, they were puzzled to find Wendy asleep on the window seat. "Oh, mother! We're back!" she said when they woke her. "All except the Lost Boys. They weren't quite ready to grow up. That's why they went back to Never Land. But I am," she blurted out.

Her parents were completely confused. "Uh... 'am'?" her father said.

"Ready to grow up," Wendy explained. She told them all about Tinker Bell, and the mermaids, and being saved by Peter Pan, and calling Captain Hook a codfish until Mr. Darling concluded that perhaps she wasn't ready to grow up after all.

"Perhaps we were a bit hasty," he said as he turned to leave the room. "I'm going to bed."

"He really is wonderful, isn't he?" Wendy said as she looked out the window. "See how well he sails the ship?"

Mrs. Darling glanced in the direction of Wendy's gaze. Then she called for her husband to take a look. Mr. Darling stared at the ship for quite a long time. Finally, he said, "You know, I have the strangest feeling that I've seen that ship before... a long time ago, when I was very young."

Madame Adelaide Bonfamille was a charming elderly lady who lived in Paris. She was extremely rich, and she had no children, so instead she spoiled her cats. They drank only cream, and ate the finest food, and slept on velvet cushions.

Duchess had been with Madame Bonfamille a long time. She was a pale, elegant feline of impeccable pedigree.

Duchess had three kittens. Little Marie looked very much like her mother. Her brothers were Berlioz, the grey one, and Toulouse, who was a burnt orange colour.

All three kittens showed unusual talents in the arts. Berlioz played the piano, and Marie sang beautifully. Toulouse was a painter. He preferred the abstract school. Duchess was very proud of all three of them.

One day, Madame Bonfamille sent for her attorney, Georges Hautecourt. Mr. Hautecourt was not as spry as he had been at age eighty, and his eyes were not as sharp as they had been, either. But he was an old and dear friend, and Madame Bonfamille trusted him completely.

"Adelaide, my dear," the attorney said, bending to kiss her hand and instead taking hold of Duchess's tail. "Ah, still the softest hands in all of Paris."

The two chatted about old times. Then Madame Bonfamille came to the point. "I want to make my will," she said. "As you know, I have no living relatives, and naturally, I want my beloved cats to be always well cared for, and certainly no one can do this better than my faithful servant, Edgar."

"You mean to say you're leaving your vast fortune to Edgar?" the attorney asked. Even her art treasures, and her jewels, and her country chateau?

"No, no, Georges, to my cats," Madame Bonfamille explained. "I wish the cats to inherit first. Then, at the end of their life spans, my entire estate will be turned over to Edgar."

Unbeknownst to Madame Bonfamille, Edgar had been eavesdropping through the voice tube. As soon as he heard about the cats, Edgar gasped. How could she do this to him?

Edgar did some rapid calculations. Each cat would live about twelve years, and since each cat has nine lives, that would be... "Anyway, it's much longer than I'd ever live," he concluded.

Besides, he had served Madame Bonfamille faithfully for years. Imagine putting the cats first! He had to think of a way to get rid of them, so he could inherit. "There are a million reasons why I should do this," he said, his eyes lighting up. "All of them dollars."

One of Edgar's daily tasks was to prepare a nightcap of warm milk for the cats. That night, he stirred some sleeping pills into it.

"Your favourite dish, prepared in a very special way," he told the cats. "Sleep well... er, I mean, eat. Eat well, of course."

"Umm. This is yummy," the cats agreed, lapping it up.

A little while later, after Madame Bonfamille had gone to bed, Edgar went to check on the cats. They were sleeping so soundly that he was able to pack them into a basket without waking them.

Edgar loaded the basket of cats into the sidecar of his motorcycle, and headed out into the countryside. His plan was simple. He would leave the cats somewhere so far from home they would never find their way back.

But Edgar had not counted on two dogs named Napoleon and Lafayette. Their hobby was chasing cars. Actually, they chased anything with wheels... bicycles, scooters... but they hadn't had a motorcycle yet that day.

When Edgar saw the dogs hurtling towards him, he tried to turn around and head the other way. Instead he lost control, and skidded down a riverbank. Then he hit a bump, and the basket of cats flew off the sidecar and rolled down the slope. The dogs continued their wild chase following Edgar up, down — and even upside down! — until all three were far out of sight.

Luckily, the basket stopped rolling before it landed in the river.

Duchess and the kittens finally awoke and looked around in confusion.

It was raining, and the cats were cold and wet. Toulouse was the only one who had any idea how they had come to be in their current predicament. But when he told his mother that he had seen Edgar driving them to the countryside on a motorcyle, Duchess said he was being ridiculous. She was sure Edgar would never do such a thing.

In Paris, the storm woke Madame Bonfamille. She went to comfort the kittens. But when she pulled back the covers, the cats' bed was empty. "They're gone!" she cried.

Her cry woke Roquefort the mouse, who lived in the wall of Madame's house. Roquefort was a good friend to Duchess and her kittens. "I've just got to find them!" he decided, and hurried out into the rain.

Duchess's friend Frou Frou the horse waited anxiously until Roquefort returned the next morning. "I've been so worried," she said. "Did you have any luck?"

"Not a sign of them, Frou Frou," Roquefort replied. "And I searched all night."

Duchess was awakened from a cold and fretful sleep by the sound of someone singing. It was a big orange alley cat named O'Malley. As soon as he heard Duchess was in trouble, he offered to help. "Helping beautiful damsels in distress is my specialty," he said.

O'Malley arranged a lift to Paris in a milk lorry. But the driver turned them out when they were only part way there, so they set out to walk the rest of the way.

Their route took them across a railway bridge. But before they reached the far side, a train rumbled toward them. The cats had to hide underneath the tracks, on the bridge supports.

The train passing overhead made a terrifying noise. So at first, no one noticed that one kitten was missing. Then Duchess heard a small voice cry, "Mama!"

Duchess looked down into the river. Marie had fallen in, and was bobbing downstream.

"Keep your head up, Marie!" O'Malley shouted. "Here I come."

He dived bravely off the bridge. In a few seconds, he reached Marie, and dragged her towards the bank, where Duchess was waiting. But then the current carried O'Malley on down the river. "I'm all right, honey. Don't worry. I'll see you downstream," he called.

Farther down the river, a couple of geese noticed O'Malley floating towards them, hanging onto a log. "Fancy that. A cat learning how to swim," Abigail said.

Abigail and Amelia went into the river to give O'Malley a swimming lesson, and nearly drowned him in the process. But eventually they got the soggy cat on dry land.

"Look, Mama! There he is!" Berlioz cried. The kittens and their mother ran to greet O'Malley and quickly made the acquaintance of the two geese, who were on holiday from England.

The kittens had never seen a goose before. "Look, Mama! They got rubber feet," Berlioz remarked.

It turned out that the geese were also on their way to Paris, so they walked the rest of the way together. By the time they reached the outskirts of the city, and went their separate ways, it was getting dark.

"Mama, I'm tired," Marie said. Berlioz was tired too, and his paws hurt. Toulouse felt as if he had walked a hundred miles.

Duchess knew the kittens couldn't travel any farther that night. O'Malley suggested a place they could stay. "It's not exactly the Ritz," he said, "but it's peaceful and quiet, and you'll..."

Then he heard the sound of jazz. "Oh, no! Sounds like Scat Cat and his gang have dropped by. Maybe we'd better find another place." But Duchess wanted to meet his friends.

Scat Cat and his buddies were great jazz musicians from all over the world. The kittens danced until they could barely keep their eyes open. It was late in the night when Duchess finally put them to bed.

Once the kittens were tucked in (or at least their mother thought they were), O'Malley and Duchess sat together in the moonlight, talking about their day. O'Malley suggested that perhaps he and Duchess should team up for good. "The kittens need a father around," he said shyly.

But although Duchess liked the idea, she was worried about Madame Bonfamille. She and the kittens would have to go home tomorrow.

The next morning, O'Malley helped Duchess and her kittens find Madame Bonfamille's house. Then it was time to say goodbye. "I don't know what to say..." Duchess stammered. "I'll never forget you, Thomas O'Malley."

Meanwhile, from his window perch, Roquefort the mouse had seen the cats arrive home. Roquefort had never stopped looking for his friends. That morning, he and Frou Frou had realised that Edgar was behind the disappearance.

So while the kittens meowed at the door for someone to let them in, the loyal mouse rapped frantically on the window to warn them. "Don't come in! Look out for Edgar," he shouted. But they couldn't hear him through the glass. They thought he was just waving hello.

So the cats were not prepared for what happened next. As soon as they stepped through the door, Edgar threw a sack over them.

Roquefort raced for help. He was out of breath when he finally caught up with O'Malley. "Duchess... kittens... in trouble," he managed to say. "The butler did it!"

O'Malley knew he couldn't rescue Duchess on his own. "You go get Scat Cat and his gang of alley cats," he told Roquefort. The mouse was reluctant to set foot in a cats' den. But O'Malley promised he would be all right, and Duchess was Roquefort's best friend, so he screwed up his courage.

Unfortunately, the cats were in a hungry mood. They teased Roquefort and frightened him a little. Then he remembered to mention O'Malley's name. It worked like magic. The cats were on their way.

Meanwhile, in the stables at Madame Bonfamille's house, Edgar was putting the sack of cats into a steamer trunk. "Now, my little pets, you're going to travel first class," he chortled. "All the way to Timbuktu." He had just locked the trunk when O'Malley pounced.

Edgar recovered quickly from the surprise attack, and was soon able to pin O'Malley against the wall. Then he tried to escape out the stable door, but when he opened it, Scat Cat and his friends burst in. They swarmed over him, their sharp claws ready for battle.

Roquefort followed close behind the cats and he looked around the stable for Duchess and the kittens. "Over there! They're in the trunk," O'Malley shouted.

Luckily, Roquefort was able to open the lock, and O'Malley hopped into the trunk. Duchess was so glad to see him! But this was no time for chatting. "Everybody out of here fast," O'Malley said.

Edgar tried to slam the trunk lid shut on O'Malley and Duchess, but Frou Frou had joined the fray. First she knocked Edgar off balance. Then she kicked up her heels and gave him a boot that sent him flying headfirst into the trunk.

By the time the movers arrived a few minutes later, the animals had Edgar safely locked away. "This must be the trunk," the driver said.

"Yup. And she goes all the way to Timbuktu," his helper said.

Madame Bonfamille never did find out exactly what had happened to Edgar. She assumed he had left his job, and disappeared. So she sent for her old friend Georges Hautecourt. He would have to revise the will.

"You know, Georges, if Edgar had only known about the will, I'm sure he never would have left," Madame Bonfamille said. Duchess and O'Malley smiled at each other.

Madame Bonfamille wasn't sure where O'Malley had come from, either, but she thought he was very handsome. "Shall we keep him?" she asked.

"Meow!" said the kittens.

So Madame Bonfamille had her will rewritten. Now, instead of Edgar, it would include O'Malley, as well as the kittens he and Duchess would have.

She added something else, too... a foundation that would provide homes for all the alley cats of Paris. Now Scat Cat and his pals really had something to sing about!

# Aladdin

Once, in a faraway land, there was a boy who lived in the streets.

The boy's name was Aladdin. Aladdin was a handsome young thief who lived by his wits in the marketplace of Agrabah. He and his pet monkey, Abu, took only what they needed to survive. And often, Aladdin gave away the food he stole to people even hungrier than he was. But he knew that one day, life would be better. "Just you wait, Abu," he said.

Aladdin had no way of knowing that in the desert, a magical cave full of treasures was waiting for him. The Tiger God had decreed it.

Not far from the marketplace where Aladdin spent his days, there was a lovely girl who lived an entirely different sort of life.

Princess Jasmine was the Sultan's daughter. She lived a life of privilege in a sumptuous palace, and had a rare tiger as her personal pet.

But time was running out for Princess Jasmine. "It's the law," the Sultan insisted. "You must marry a prince by your next birthday. And it will be your birthday in three days."

The trouble was, Jasmine did not love the prince her father had picked out for her to marry.

"What shall I do?" she asked her tiger, Rajah. She could think of only one solution. She disguised herself in the clothing of an ordinary citizen, and ran away from home.

Princess Jasmine had never been alone outside the palace walls. She found the bustle of the marketplace strange and a little scary. She didn't even know that ordinary people had to pay for things. She found out, though, when she took an apple from a fruit stand and gave it to a hungry child.

"You'd better be able to pay for that!" the fruit merchant yelled.

But before Jasmine could come to any harm, Aladdin appeared out of the gathering crowd, and rescued the frightened girl. "Forgive her. She's my poor sister. She's a little crazy in the head," Aladdin explained.

Aladdin grabbed Jasmine's hand, and led her to the peace and safety of his favourite rooftop, far above the streets. That's when she told him she had run away from home, because her father was going to make her marry someone she didn't love.

"Wow! That's awful!" Aladdin agreed when he had heard the whole story. Well, not quite the whole story. Jasmine didn't bother to mention that she was the Sultan's daughter. So it was perfectly natural for Aladdin to hope that one day Jasmine might love him.

Meanwhile, the Sultan had fallen under the spell of his evil adviser, Jafar.

For years, Jafar had been trying to lay his hands on a magic lamp that was hidden in the Cave of Wonders. So far, all his schemes had failed. So now he wanted the Sultan's Mystic Blue Diamond.

"You will give me the diamond!" Jafar said, holding his hypnotic cobra staff before the Sultan's eyes.

"Yes, master," the Sultan replied.

With the diamond now in his possession, Jafar was able to carry out the next step in his plan. "Our moment draws near, Iago!" he told his parrot. "With this diamond, I can find..."

"A husband for Jasmine?" asked the parrot.

"No, fool! The one who can get us the lamp!"

Jafar knew that the Sultan's diamond had the power to bring to life the all-seeing Sands of Time. "Show me the one who can enter the cave!" he commanded to the hourglass containing the sands.

The answer was... Aladdin.

Jafar dispatched the palace guards to Aladdin's rooftop hiding place, and had him arrested.

"Release him at once!" Jasmine ordered, throwing back her hood so the guards could recognise her. But the guards did not dare disobey Jafar.

When Aladdin was caught, he was thrown into a dungeon. At first he could think only about Jasmine. The guards had called her a princess. "A princess! I can't believe it!" he said to Abu.

But then Jafar arrived, disguised as an ancient prisoner. He offered to help Aladdin escape. "I need a pair of young, strong legs like yours, to go into the cave and help me get a worthless lamp," Jafar said. "The rest of the treasure can be yours."

Of course, Aladdin agreed.

That night, in the desert, the head of the Tiger God rose slowly from the sands before Aladdin's astonished eyes. The tiger's mouth created a huge cave.

"Who disturbs my slumber?" the voice of the cave thundered.

"It is I — Aladdin," the boy replied.

"Proceed," the voice boomed. "Touch nothing but the lamp."

As Aladdin and Abu entered the cave, Jafar cried after them, "Remember — fetch the lamp, and then you shall have your reward!"

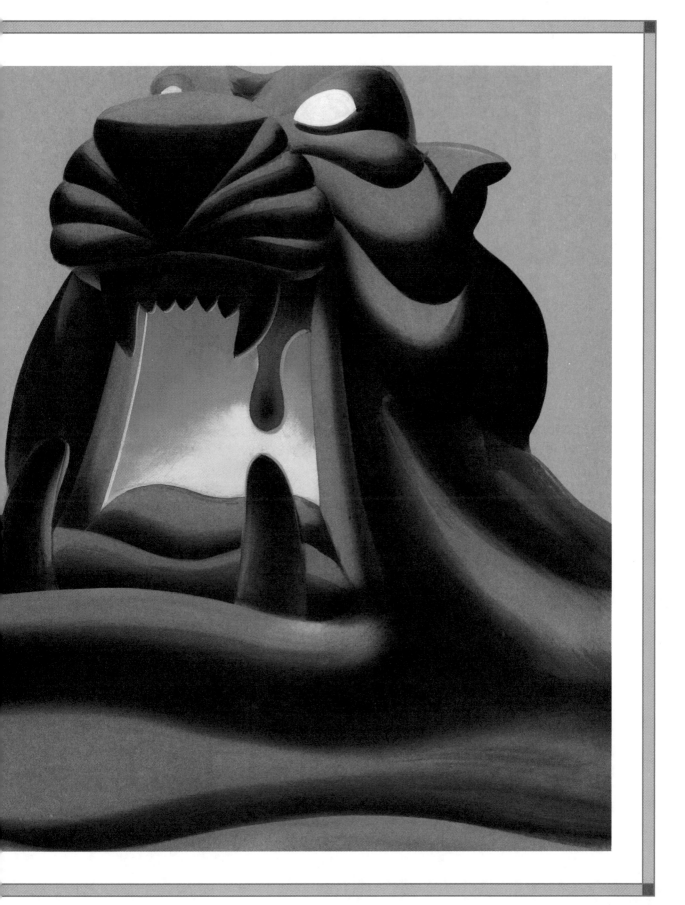

Aladdin and Abu followed a golden staircase down, down to a chamber filled with glittering treasure. There was so much gold that it cast an eerie glow.

Abu could never resist shiny things. He reached for a sparkling jewel. "No, Abu. We mustn't touch anything until we find the lamp," Aladdin warned.

They noticed a magic carpet peeking out from behind a heap of gold. Abu was afraid of it, but it showed them the way to a second chamber, where the lamp was hidden.

But Abu could not resist the glitter any longer. He grabbed a huge ruby. The cave trembled.

"You have touched the forbidden treasure. Now you will never again see the light of day!" the huge voice roared.

The cave began to fill with molten lava. Aladdin pulled Abu to safety on the Magic Carpet just in time.

The carpet sped them to the mouth of the cave, where Jafar waited. "Help us!" Aladdin called, clinging to the rocks.

"Throw me the lamp!" Jafar replied. He snatched it from Aladdin's hand, then pulled out a dagger, aiming to strike the boy.

"What are you doing?" Aladdin cried.

In a flash, Abu had sunk his teeth into Jafar's arm. Jafar screamed, and dropped the dagger. But Aladdin and Abu fell back into the cave.

Finally, the cave stopped shaking and became as silent as a tomb. "We're trapped in here," Aladdin despaired.

Abu chirped and held up his paw, revealing the lamp. "Why, you hairy little thief!" Aladdin laughed when he realised the monkey had grabbed the lamp from Jafar.

When Aladdin tried to rub some of the dust off, the lamp began to glow, and a towering column of smoke poured out of its spout.

"Say, you're a lot smaller than my last master," the giant shape said.

"Are you the genie of the lamp?" Aladdin asked.

"The one and only!" the Genie replied.

Aladdin was dumbfounded. Still, he was used to thinking quickly.

"If you were a real genie, you could get us out of this cave!" he challenged. Instantly, they were back above ground.

"I guess you're a genie all right!" Aladdin said. "Do I get three wishes?"

"Of course!" the Genie said.

Aladdin thought of Princess Jasmine. "I wish to be a prince!" he declared as his first wish.

The people of Agrabah had never seen such a splendid procession. Even Aladdin's closest friends would never have guessed the true identity of the handsome prince dressed in shining silks.

"Prince Ali Ababwa," the palace guard announced as Aladdin flew into the throne room on the Magic Carpet.

"Your majesty, I have journeyed from afar to seek your daughter's hand in marriage," Aladdin said to the astonished Sultan.

395

That night, Aladdin took Jasmine for a ride on his flying carpet. That's when she discovered he was the same kind young man she had met in the marketplace. Before the evening was over, she knew Aladdin was the one she wanted to marry.

Meanwhile, Jafar had already decided to marry the princess himself. He thought that was the only way he could prevent her from making trouble for him.

As soon as Aladdin returned from his evening out with Jasmine, Jafar ordered the palace guards to seize him. Aladdin soon found himself bound and gagged, and then thrown from a cliff into the sea.

Aladdin struggled to free one hand from the ropes, and was barely able to rub the lamp.

"I'm sure that you wish I'd get you out of this mess," the Genie said when he appeared.

Meanwhile, in the palace, Jasmine was telling her father that she wanted to marry Prince Ali. But Jafar had cast another spell on the Sultan. "You will wed Jafar," the Sultan droned to his daughter.

"Never!" the princess cried. "Father, what's wrong with you?"

"I know!" Aladdin shouted from the doorway. He seized the hypnotic staff from Jafar, and smashed it to pieces.

Jafar quickly fled to his chambers, and began plotting his next move. He knew he was up against a powerful opponent. The charming Prince Ali, it seemed, was really Aladdin. Furthermore, during the scuffle over the cobra staff, Jafar had glimpsed the Genie's magic lamp hidden in Aladdin's robes.

So that night, Jafar sent his devious parrot, Iago, to steal the lamp from Aladdin's room.

Jafar gloated with pleasure as he finally rubbed the lamp he had coveted for so long. "I am now your master!" he exclaimed when the Genie appeared.

The Genie was not too pleased with this new development. Still, he had to obey.

"I wish to be Sultan," Jafar commanded.

At that very moment, the Sultan was announcing to the people of Agrabah the engagement of his daughter, Jasmine, to Prince Ali. But in the middle of his speech, the crowd gasped in horror. Their beloved Sultan had vanished, and Jafar stood before them in the Sultan's robes.

"We will never bow to you!" Aladdin said defiantly.

"Then you will cower!" Jafar replied, rubbing the lamp. This time, he told the Genie he wanted to be the most powerful sorcerer in the world.

"I don't like it, but you've got it, Master!" the Genie replied.

As his first trick, the new sorcerer banished Aladdin to the ends of the world. Aladdin found himself in a land of ice and snow.

"How will I ever get out of here?" he groaned. Then he and Abu discovered that the Magic Carpet had been transported with them. They flew back towards the palace.

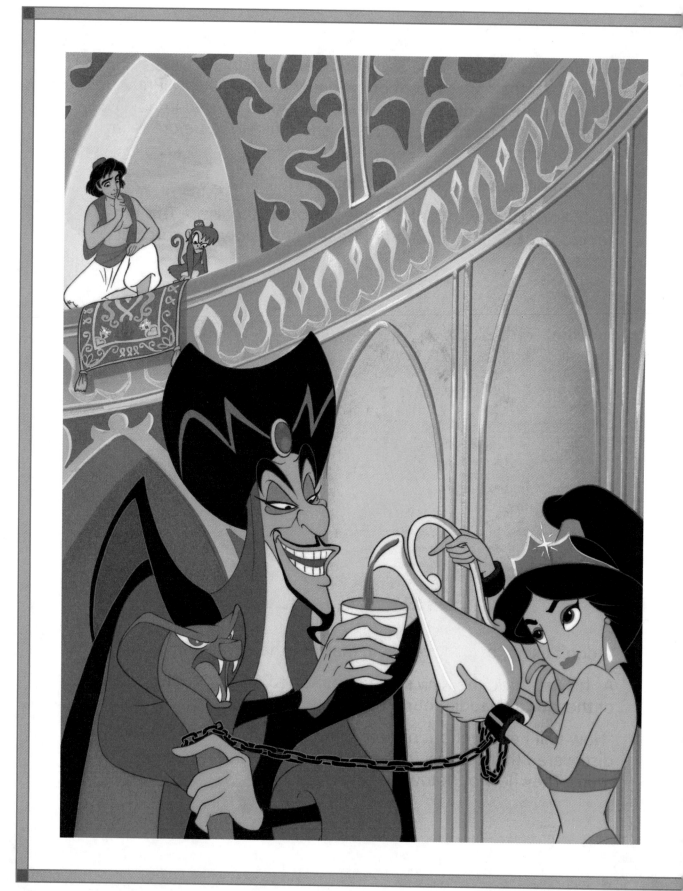

Jafar, meanwhile, had taken over the Sultan's palace and was forcing Jasmine to cater to his every wish. "Bring me more wine!" he ordered. As she did, Jasmine caught a glimpse of Aladdin and Abu hiding on the balcony. She secretly signalled to Aladdin who crept up behind Jafar and attacked him.

Jafar fought back with his evil magic. Soon he imprisoned Jasmine in an hourglass which rapidly began filling with sand.

Then, turning back toward Aladdin, Jafar snarled. "How many times do I have to get rid of you, boy?" And with one wave of his hand, the sorcerer surrounded himself with a wall of flame.

"Are you afraid to fight me, you cowardly snake?" asked Aladdin.

"A snake, am I?" Jafar replied. "So be it!" Instantly, Jafar turned himself into a huge cobra.

"Did you think you could outwit the most powerful sorcerer on earth?" the cobra hissed, preparing to strike.

Aladdin thought quickly. "The Genie has more power than you'll ever have, Jafar," he said.

"You're right!" Jafar said. He seized the lamp in his coils, and rubbed. "Genie, my third wish is to be... a genie!" The cobra vanished, replaced by a huge genie shouting, "Now I have absolute power!"

In the commotion, Aladdin quickly took the
opportunity to free Jasmine from the hourglass.
Then he grabbed the lamp and sucked Jafar the
"genie" inside it.

Later, with Jafar imprisoned in the lamp, Aladdin
decided on his third and final wish. He used it to
free his friend, the Genie, forever.

And although Aladdin was sad to say good-bye
to his good friend, he soon found reason to
celebrate — the Sultan decided to change the law
so that Princess Jasmine could marry anyone she
wished. And that's what she did. She chose
Aladdin.

# ALICE
## *in*
## WONDERLAND

411

Alice's older sister was reading aloud. It was a very dull story, the history of King William something-or-other, so to amuse herself Alice made a daisy crown for her cat Dinah. Her sister looked up from the book, and gave Alice a stern look. "Will you kindly pay attention to your history lesson?" she said.

Alice tried, but she just couldn't seem to keep her mind on it. "In my world, the books would be nothing but pictures," she said, half to herself.

It was a lovely idea, really. A world all of her own. "Everything would be nonsense," she said. Dinah nodded thoughtfully.

Alice lay down in the long grass, and thought about it some more. Her sister's voice was making her drowsy. "You'd be just like people, Dinah. And all the other animals, too," Alice continued.

It was then that the White Rabbit rushed by. "Oh, my fur and whiskers!" the rabbit cried, looking at his pocket watch. "I'm late! I'm late! I'm late!"

"Now, this is curious. What could a rabbit possibly be late for?" Alice wondered. "Sir!" she called after him.

"No time to say 'hello'. Good-bye!" the rabbit replied.

"It must be something awfully important. Like a party or something," Alice decided.

She followed the rabbit to a hole at the base of a large tree, and peered in. "What a peculiar place to have a party. You know, Dinah, we really shouldn't be doing this," Alice said as she squeezed through the hole. "After all, we haven't been invited, and curiosity often leads to trouble..."

Dinah could barely hear the last few words, because Alice was vanishing from sight down a deep hole. "Good-bye, Dinah!" she called. Fortunately, her skirt ballooned out, and kept her from falling too quickly. She had time to observe the odd collection of items on the walls — lamps and mirrors and end tables and...

"Oh!" Alice said as she landed with a thud.

Alice looked around. The White Rabbit was nearing the end of a long hallway. "Wait! Please!" Alice cried. But he didn't, so she followed.

At the end of the hallway was a door. She opened it, and found another smaller door, then another even smaller, too small for her to get through. "Why don't you try the bottle on the table?" the doorknob suggested.

The label on the bottle read "Drink me," and the contents tasted like cherry tart and roast turkey. "Goodness!" Alice cried when she realised she had shrunk smaller than the bottle.

But at least she was now the right size to fit through the door. "I forgot to tell you," the doorknob said. "I'm locked."

The key was on top of the table, far above Alice's reach. "Whatever will I do?" she asked.

"Try the box," the doorknob suggested.

She hadn't noticed the box before. It contained a biscuit with "Eat Me" written on it. "All right," Alice said, taking a few bites. Immediately, she began to grow, and kept growing until her head hit the ceiling. All at once Alice began to cry, and couldn't seem to stop. The floor was awash with tears. "The bottle!" the doorknob cried. Alice grabbed it, and took a sip.

The next thing she knew, Alice was small again, had fallen into the bottle, and was floating along on a river of tears. "I wish I hadn't cried so much!" she said.

There were a great number of creatures on the river, having some sort of race. Alice asked for help from a passing Dodo, but he was too busy making nautical remarks.

Then Alice caught another glimpse of the White Rabbit, and followed him into the woods. But instead of the White Rabbit, she found two odd little fellows named Tweedledee and Tweedledum, who told her a long, sad story about a walrus and a carpenter and some oysters. Alice crept away before they could tell her another one.

Farther along, Alice came upon a small neat house. Just as soon as she said, "I wonder who lives here," the White Rabbit appeared.

"Mary Ann! What are you doing out here?" the rabbit asked Alice. "Don't just do something, stand there! Go and get my gloves!"

"Goodness! I suppose I'll be taking orders from Dinah next," Alice said. All the same, she went into the house and started looking. "Now if I were a rabbit, where would I keep my gloves?" she wondered aloud.

She looked in the biscuit jar and saw another biscuit labelled "Eat me," so she did. "Oh no! Not again!" Alice cried as her head hit the ceiling.

The White Rabbit came running. "Now look here, Mary Ann!" he said. But when Alice's giant foot bumped into him, he went running in the other direction. "Help! Assistance! A monster!" he cried.

By now, Alice had grown so large that parts of her were sticking out through the doors and windows. She was trapped.

The White Rabbit soon came back with the Dodo. "Do something," the rabbit said.

The Dodo thought for a minute, then hit on an idea. "We'll burn the house down!" he said.

"What!?" said the White Rabbit, thinking about all his lovely furniture.

"Oh, no!" Alice cried. "This is serious!" Then she spotted the rabbit's garden. "Perhaps if I ate something," she thought.

She reached for a carrot, but the White Rabbit got in the way, and ended up dangling from her fingers, holding the carrot.

"I'm sorry, but I simply must eat something," Alice explained.

"Not me, you barbarian!" the rabbit cried as Alice lifted the carrot towards her mouth.

She took a bite, and began shrinking. But by the time she was small again, the White Rabbit had remembered his appointment and disappeared into the woods. "Wait, please!" Alice cried.

Alice had grown far too small to keep up with the White Rabbit. She was so small that flowers towered over her head. Then a butterfly flew past, and another. But there was something odd about them. "What curious butterflies!" Alice exclaimed.

"You mean bread-and-butterflies," a voice corrected.

The voice seemed to come from a rose. "But that's nonsense. Flowers can't talk," Alice said.

"Of course, we can..." a rose replied.

"...if there's anyone worth talking to," an iris explained.

But when the flowers heard that Alice was not a flower, they asked her to move along. "We don't want weeds in our bed," the pansies said. Thinking the flowers could learn a few things about manners, Alice continued on her way.

On the other side of the flower bed, Alice noticed some clouds shaped like letters. In fact, they were made of smoke, and were being blown by a large green caterpillar lying on a mushroom. "Who are you?" the Caterpillar asked in a very slow voice.

"Why, I hardly know, Sir," Alice said. "I've changed so many times since this morning, you see."

"I do not see. Explain yourself," the Caterpillar said, but then he lost interest in her explanation. Instead, he made Alice learn a poem. "How doth the little crocodile improve his shining tail?" he instructed.

Afterwards, the Caterpillar disappeared in a cloud of smoke, and turned into a butterfly. Alice decided it was time to leave. But the Butterfly called her back. "One side will make you grow taller," he said.

"One side of what?" said Alice.

"And the other side will make you grow shorter," he said.

"The other side of what?" Alice asked again.

"The mushroom, of course," the Butterfly said before flying away.

Alice carefully broke off a piece from each side of the mushroom, and examined them. They looked identical. Which was which?

She nibbled one piece, and immediately shot up until her head was higher than the highest trees.

"Help! A serpent!" a bird screamed.

"I'm not a serpent. I'm just a little girl," Alice said.

"Little! Ha!" the bird replied. The bird was still squawking when Alice took a bite from the other piece of mushroom.

In seconds, she was small again. Too small, actually. She studied the pieces again. "I wonder if I'll ever get the knack of it," she said. Carefully, she licked one piece until she was the size she wanted to be. Then she put both pieces in her pockets, just in case.

"Now, let's see. Where was I?" Alice said. The signs at the crossroads were no help. They pointed in every direction.

Then she heard someone singing, and spotted a pair of eyes and some shining teeth on a branch above her head. Very slowly, the rest of the body emerged into view. "Why, you're a cat!" Alice said.

"A Cheshire Cat," the cat replied before he faded away again. All that was left was a grin. Alice found it so unsettling that she was barely able to ask which direction she should go. "That depends on where you want to get to," the Cheshire Cat said.

"It really doesn't matter," Alice replied.

"Then it really doesn't matter which way you go," the Cheshire Cat said. "However, if I were looking for a White Rabbit, I'd ask the Mad Hatter."

So Alice followed the sign to the Mad Hatter's.

The Mad Hatter and his friend the March Hare were in the middle of an unbirthday party when Alice arrived. It looked to Alice as if there was plenty of room at the table, but when she tried to sit down, the March Hare shouted, "No room!" and told her she was being very rude for coming without an invitation.

Alice quickly apologised. "I'm very sorry, but I did enjoy your singing..." she began to say.

As it turned out, the Hatter and the Hare almost never received compliments about their singing. So they changed their minds and invited Alice to join them. And since she didn't know what an unbirthday was, the Mad Hatter explained. Only one day of the year was one's birthday, he said. Therefore, the other 364 days were unbirthdays.

"Why, then today is my unbirthday too!" Alice said.

So Alice was given her own unbirthday cake with a candle to blow out. Then the Dormouse residing in the teapot recited a poem in her honour.

But Alice never did receive the cup of tea she had been offered. The Hatter and the Hare were too busy telling nonsensical riddles, and changing chairs every few minutes. Then the White Rabbit dropped by. But instead of offering him cake, the Hatter and the Hare poured tea and sugar into his pocket watch, then tossed him over the wall.

"This is the stupidest tea party I've ever been to in all my life," Alice declared, and left.

"I've had enough nonsense," Alice decided. "I'm going home!"

The only problem was, she couldn't find the way, and the harder she looked, the more lost she became. Finally she decided to sit down, and wait for someone to find her.

It wasn't long before the Cheshire Cat appeared. He was not at all surprised to hear she could not find her way. "That's because you have no way," he explained. "All the ways are the Queen's ways."

Alice would simply have to meet the Queen, he said. He opened a door in a large tree. Through the door was a garden maze, and Alice heard voices singing. Alice walked towards the sound. It was coming from three playing cards, singing happily while they slopped red paint onto white roses.

"Why must you paint them red?" Alice asked.

The cards explained that they had accidentally planted white roses, but the Queen had wanted red roses. So they were quickly painting them red to avoid punishment.

"Goodness," Alice said.

Alice was helping the cards with their painting when she heard the sound of a trumpet. "The Queen!" the cards shouted, and quickly hid their ladders and brushes.

Then Alice noticed a row of marching cards approaching, led by none other than the White Rabbit.

"Her Royal Majesty, the Queen of Hearts," the White Rabbit announced. And then, in a quieter voice, he added, "And the King."

The Queen had come to inspect her gardens, and it took her only a second to notice something odd about the roses. She touched one. "Who's been painting my roses red?" she shouted. "Someone will lose his head!"

The guilty cards were quickly rounded up and marched away. Then the Queen turned her attention to Alice.

As soon as she realised Alice was a little girl, and not a playing card, she offered her all sorts of grown-up advice. "Speak nicely," she said, "and don't twiddle your fingers. Turn out your toes. Curtsy. Open your mouth a little wider. And always say 'Yes, Your Majesty'."

"Yes, Your Majesty," Alice said. Then she tried to ask the way home.

"I'll ask the questions," the Queen insisted. "Do you play croquet?"

Alice did, so she was ordered to join in a game. But it was the strangest game of croquet she had ever played! The mallets were flamingos, the ball was a hedgehog, and the hoops were playing cards.

What was worse, the game wasn't fair. The playing card hoops ran wherever necessary to make sure that the Queen always won her shots. Meanwhile, Alice's mallet hung as limp as a piece of spaghetti.

Alice was losing badly, until the Cheshire Cat appeared again. He thought it would be fun to make the Queen really angry. And he did, too, by tipping her upside down.

The Queen didn't see who did it. "Someone's head will roll for this!" she said, looking straight at Alice. "Yours!"

Fortunately, the King had a soft spot for Alice. "Couldn't she have a trial first?" he asked his wife. "Just a little trial?"

"Very well, then," the Queen said.

The members of the jury listened carefully as the White Rabbit read out the charges against Alice. She was accused of luring the Queen into a game of croquet, and then making her lose her temper.

The Queen was also the judge, and she wanted to pronounce a sentence right away. But the King convinced her to call a few witnesses first. So the March Hare was called, and the Dormouse, and the Mad Hatter. But they only managed to get jam on the Queen, and make things worse for Alice. "Off with her head!" the Queen cried.

That's when Alice remembered the mushrooms, and popped pieces of both into her mouth. "I'm not afraid of you!" Alice cried, towering over the courtroom. "You're nothing but a pack of cards!

"And as for you, Your Majesty..." Alice continued, wagging her finger at the Queen. But by now the other piece of mushroom had taken effect, and Alice was growing tiny. "You're just a fat, pompous, bad-tempered old tyrant!"

Alice said the last part a bit nervously, for she had just realised how small she suddenly was.

"What were you saying, my dear?" the Queen said. She leaned down over Alice with a wicked smile. To Alice, the Queen's head looked absolutely huge. Her mouth was as big as a cave. And for some reason, the Cheshire Cat was sitting on top of her crown. Alice put her hands over her face, and shook her head.

"She simply said that you're a fat, pompous, bad-tempered old tyrant!" she heard the Cheshire Cat repeat.

"Off with her head!" the Queen shouted. Playing cards swarmed over Alice.

Alice fled through the garden maze, the playing cards following in a long line behind her. "Off with her head!" she could hear the Queen hollering.

"Just a moment! You can't leave a tea party without having a cup of tea," the Mad Hatter shouted.

"But I can't stop now!" Alice cried over her shoulder.

"We insist!" the March Hare called.

Alice sneaked a look backwards. They were all following her: the King and Queen, Tweedledum and Tweedledee, the Walrus and the Carpenter... "I simply must get out!" Alice cried, twisting the doorknob on the tiny door.

"But you are outside," the doorknob replied. "See for yourself!"

"Alice, wake up!" she heard a voice calling. It was her sister. Alice turned restlessly, and hugged her cat closer.

"Alice! Will you kindly pay attention and recite your lesson," her sister said.

"What?" Alice said and jumped to her feet. "How doth the little crocodile improve his shining tail," she recited.

"Alice! What are you talking about?" her sister said.

Alice tried to explain. "The Caterpillar said..."

"Caterpillar! For goodness sake!" her sister said. "Well, come along, it's time for tea."

So Alice picked up Dinah, and followed her sister, feeling quite content to be back in a familiar place with her own little cat and a clear path home.